DON'T COUNT THAT CHICKEN

'til your fingers need lickin'

J. Micheal Unrue

MYRIAD PUBLISHING
Greenville, South Carolina

This book is a work of fiction. Names, characters, places and incidents, either are the product of the author's imagination or are used fictitiously, and any resemblance to actual persons, living or dead, events or locales is entirely coincidental.

So there.

ISBN 0-9648969-0-7

Cover Design by I. Riedel

For Caitlin, Sara & Rebecca

ONE

My name is Jimmy Nance. Well actually it's James Madison Nance, after our fourth President. I've got a brother named James, too—James Monroe Nance. People call me Jimmy and him Monroe to cut down on the confusion. I asked Mama about it once and she said that it was okay to name two sons the same thing as long as they were named after different people.

I'm one of the good guys. I'm kind to people even when they're not kind to me, and Ernie my cat thinks I'm the best thing on two legs, except maybe for my girlfriend Charlotte, who is the joy and sorrow of my life. But I'll save that for later.

I hate to be so prefatorial but there's something I've got to tell you and I'm not looking forward to it because I already know how you're going to react. But since it's germane to the business at hand, well I gotta.

I'm an Investigator for the I.R.S. here in Atlanta.

Should I wait until you calm down or just go on?

Now most folks think that all we do is hassle the millions of poor, struggling working people in this country in the hope of squeezing more out of them. That's only part of it.

The other part is the Investigative Branch, which tries to ferret out the people who either pay very little tax, despite obvious income, or who don't bother to file at all. And if you'd stop and think a minute before getting mad at me you might just come to the conclusion that if these folks paid their fair share the rest of us probably wouldn't have to pay as much.

Shirkers come in two categories, the high-end and the low-end.

The high-end are people like real estate developers, ball players, tax lawyers and the occasional country singer.

The Good Lord even picked a tax collector to be one of his own, which was Matthew, even though he wouldn't let him anywhere near the money, and instead let Judas handle it.

I don't know what it is about paying taxes that gets people so upset. Without taxes there would be no government. Without government there would be anarchy. Besides, you gotta believe that if *Jim Earl and the Appaloosas* hadn't got caught for shortchanging Uncle Sam and slapped with a heavy penalty they wouldn't have the number eighteen hit on the country charts today...'Stomp Me, Shoot Me, Gut Me Clean. But Darlin' Please Don't Kiss That Taxman'.

Another thing is how out-and-out silly people get about the subject. The last time I saw my brother Monroe he said,

"You know, I had a deal workin' that woulda paid me about a hundred thousand dollars but decided not to go through with it on account a taxes."

"You mean you didn't make a hundred thousand dollars because you might have had to pay twenty-five thousand or so in taxes?"

"Damn straight."

"Well what about the seventy-five thousand dollars you would've had left over?"

Monroe stared at me for a minute then spit over the porch railing, which was his way of telling me that having a Revenooer for a brother was the sorrow of his life and a God-awful embarrassment to boot.

After awhile he raised his chin toward Stone Mountain and mustered as much dignity as he could with dribble on his shirt.

"A man's gotta have principles," he said.

Which is true. I've got principles, too.

I never really wanted to be an accountant in the first place. I wanted to play basketball. I was a hell of a shot and good enough to start small college. But there were a couple of problems.

The first was that my start-up time left a lot to be desired. Once I got up a head of steam I could keep up with the best of them. The only thing is that it takes me about fifty yards to get going full-tilt. And since a basketball court is only thirty yards long, give or take a couple, I often found myself hustling in one direction while the other nine guys were hustling in the other.

But the real kicker is that I've got very small hands for a man my size. I'm six-one but have got the hands of a piano teacher, and even in college couldn't palm the ball.

It was the sorrow of my life before I met Charlotte.

I don't know how or why the Cosmos divvies up the spoils of life, but I have a natural facility with numbers. Watch this. 42% of 380 is 159.6. See what I mean?

I passed the C.P.A. exam the first time out. I was all set, except for the fact that I hated accounting. I heard that Herschel Walker was going to be an F.B.I. agent when he decided to stop running over linebackers, so I tried out for the F.B.I., thinking that by the time Herschel came along I'd have enough seniority for us to be buddies.

They put me on waivers and the dreaded I.R.S. picked up my option.

It's not a bad deal. They kick you out automatically at fifty-seven with a nifty little pension. Unfortunately, I've got twenty-six years to go. The Iron Pyrite of life.

Monroe, on the other hand, struck the Motherlode. He was a star outside linebacker at Georgia Tech, where he took his Engineering degree in something called Grits Displacement, and was drafted in the sixth round by the New Orleans Saints. He was never really what you'd call a star, but he played in the nickel package and on special teams. And he had a good lawyer who got him a contract with a guaranteed annuity if he was retired by injury any time after his seventh year.

On opening day of his eighth season he got clipped by a rookie from the Vikings and was set for life. If *Sports Illustrated* ever does an *All Time Injuries of the NFL* tape to sell subscriptions to their magazine, Monroe will be right up there with Joe Theismann.

They'd show it in slow motion and from a hundred different angles how his right foot started out on the ground pointing north, and ended up behind his left shoulder pointing southwest.

Sometimes I'll catch Monroe watching the replay all misty-eyed. But when I tell him that I think watching that thing is a little sick he just grins and says,

"Forty-eight thousand, six hundred and eleven dollars and twenty-six cents a year for life, Bubba."

Which is more than enough since he bought a house, a couple of trucks, and a boat with all the fixins with the money he earned as a player. Now he passes the time as a dabbler in small investments—a roadhouse that went under and a fish camp that didn't—and marriages—Shirley from the roadhouse, who went under with a Pepsi man from Augusta, and Shirlene from the fish camp, who went under, too, and took his favorite truck-and-boat rig with her.

As fond as I am of Monroe, he was the sorrow of my life before Charlotte or even having hands too small to palm a basketball.

After his third year in the NFL he bought Mama and Daddy a big double-wide for the hill they live on up in Bartow County. That was the same year I turned Revenooer. Mama and Daddy never said an unkind word about it, but even so, it's gotten to the point where I hate to go up there. Every time I do Mama takes me on a tour of the trailer, even though it's been there for eight years and hasn't changed a lick. And she'll clasp her hands to her breasts and let her eyes float from corner to corner and sigh out loud the way Donna Reed used to do. And I can't stand it.

The branch I work for handles the low-enders. People like petty hustlers, pool sharks, small-time drug dealers, fences and the like. Which is why I'm driving my van down the Martin Luther King, Jr. on an early Spring morning.

I work undercover, doing what little I can do to find out who some of the wrong people are and what they're up to. It's not all that complicated. If a guy drives a nice car and wears a snappy suit and mingles a lot, then he could be a salesman or he could be a pimp. Well, that's an ugly word so let's just say that all the women in his life aren't his sisters.

The fastest way to find out is to look at his tax return. If he claims he put fifty thousand business miles a year on his car then he's probably a salesman, even if he only did thirty. If he doesn't file a return at all, then odds are he buys a lot of big hats and sleeps during the day.

Something else I'll bet you didn't know is that a lot of people like me operate legitimate businesses as a cover. Sometimes it's something we've seized from somebody who didn't pay up, and sometimes it's something we've created to fit the situation. But it's important to me, at least, that you know that most of these things are profitable. That I don't just burn gas and live off the public nut. In fact, my business is thriving.

I'm a condom distributor. I've got over a hundred machines in about fifty locations scattered all over my turf, which is old Atlanta, Western Atlanta to be more specific, or sometimes affectionately referred to as the bad part of town.

Last year alone I took in enough money to not only pay my own salary and expenses, but to get a newer van and upgrade most of my machines. Not to mention give Uncle Sam a tidy profit.

My boss doesn't appreciate it, though. He says that prosperity is a great temptation. He says it just like that, too.

"Nance. Never forget that prosperity is a great temptation."

I don't much like my boss. He's a fat guy. Now I'm not talking about people with bad glands, or a crummy childhood, or some other infirmity of the heart which causes such grief. I'd never disparage a wounded soul.

But my boss isn't one of them. He's a pig. He looks like a pig. He eats like a pig. His clothes are too tight and pooch out every which way, and he sweats all the time.

And I mean perpetually.

Sometimes I wonder, especially when he's on my case, that if I tripped him in the hallway just how far he'd slide.

I love my job. The people who've got my machines in their places of business, all discreetly placed by the way, usually in the men's room although more and more ladies' rooms are adding to the decor in light of the infectious state of American courtship, are all good folks.

And I never take cheap shots. When Snuff Waldrep, who makes the best hash in Atlanta, even if there is some goat in it like people say, dips into his cash drawer and gives the missus a twenty to go to the beauty parlor, even though that money is technically income and won't ever see the light of day, I just look the other way. And not because Mrs. Waldrep bears a close resemblance to Bullwinkle, either.

Like I said, I've got principles, too. It bothers me some that they don't know I'm a Fed. So the best I can do is treat everybody as if I wasn't anything more than a pretty fair rubber man. I never hassle the little guy. I do things the right way even when it isn't my way. And when the two come in conflict, then I just do the best I can. Charlotte says I'm stubborn. But all I really care about is to someday look back over my life and know that I was a good and decent man.

What I do is keep an eye out for people who seem to lead a prosperous life but never send We The People so much as a Christmas card. And occasionally I hit paydirt.

Like last year when Flora Watkins allowed herself to be seen in several new ensembles and a silver BMW that was practically new. It was well known that Flora operated a day care center in her house, which is a very honorable and sometimes profitable profession, but hardly enough to support her new lifestyle.

So with a little snooping I come to find out that she's swapped taking care of children for taking care of grown men, and moved from daytime to twenty-four hours a day. Not to mention that she recruited a whole bunch of women who didn't look the first thing like kindergarten teachers.

My job is to file a report and then lay low. The real card-carrying R-Men come swooping in and take care of business, leaving me alone to eat a bite and run my route.

My life is good. Especially today, because it's Tuesday and on Tuesdays I eat at Rudy's. He makes something he calls his Red Bean Casserole that's enough to make you want to get naked and lay in the sun.

It's not much of a casserole, really. Just red beans and Vidalia onion baked in brown sugar gravy with some biscuit dough crust. Besides, Rudy's one of my best customers and would never let anybody trash one of my machines. He is also my friend, and the fact that I am usually the only white man in the place doesn't seem to bother him in the least.

Old Atlanta has fallen on hard times. I worry about the people who live here, and how attractive taking a shortcut can be when you're desperate.

People say the old city is dying, just like old cities everywhere in this country. That pretty soon she'll breathe her last. I disagree. I think she's just got a bad case of halitosis and only needs some strong mouthwash.

It's just like my third grade teacher, Mrs. Armbrister, who taught school until she was eighty-six, even when her mouth hurt so bad from gingivitis that she stopped wearing her dentures altogether, and which didn't affect me the least bit adversely until I got into the fifth grade and they asked me what state had St. Paul as its capital and I said *Mimmetoga*.

Her gums may be bleeding, but her heart beats true.

TWO

Rudy's is on the corner of First and Church and if you want you can sit in a booth and watch the traffic move in four different directions. I never do. I always sit at the counter and chat with Rudy. If anybody knows what's going on in this part of town it's him, although I never milk him for information or ask him about specifics. Fact is, most of the wrong people also have a mean streak and I honestly believe that people like Rudy are just as anxious to see the back of them as I am.

Rudy even claims the income from my machines, which some don't and I don't push it, not only because I have to protect my cover, but also because I figure that at least part of the reason they don't is out of sheer embarrassment.

I love going in there. He's got the ceiling fans on slow and the jukebox on slower. Right now it's B.B. King and Lucille. I carry a plain little satchel so that people who don't know what's in it won't be offended by what's in it, even though most folks in Rudy's know me and occasionally even walk up and hint around for a free sample. Most times I oblige them. It's good public relations and it's good for business, condoms being what you'd call a consumption item.

Rudy's got six machines. Three in the men's room and three in the ladies'. The stock is about the same but the machines are different. The machines in the ladies' room are plain-Jane with a big sticker on them that reads 'For The Prevention of Disease Only'. No need for a lot of hoo-ha seeing as how it's such a delicate matter.

Frankly, the machines in the men's room embarrass me, even though I keep telling myself that it's a necessity of doing business in this day and age. These machines have got pictures of real live women showing most of their body parts with just a little something here and there to make it look respectable. It isn't. In fact, I still can't bear to look at them without wondering if those girls' Daddies knew that they were in those pictures.

I try not to be too showy, either. Oh, I've got some merchanise in colors, variety not only being the spice of life but downright necessary to keep somebody from getting so bored that he just up and stops taking precautions altogether, which as we all know can be a real hazard, but on the whole my stuff is pretty tame.

I got your Regulars, which most people use, your Ribbed, which some people call French Ticklers, and which I agree might be a bit much, except that people these days seem to be more and more interested in the overall quality of their relations and these Ticklers have got more traction than a Monster Truck, and something called The Missile, which to be perfectly honest I don't want to discuss.

I refill the machines and collect the money. Over a hundred and forty dollars this week, which is good and about a third of which is profit for Uncle Sam. Sometimes I wonder if the Honorable Robert E. Rubin, who as we all know is Secretary of the Treasury, and indirectly my boss, ever stops to think that a part of the reason he can get a free haircut is because of the good people of Western Atlanta giving me their patronage.

I sit down at the counter and start to sort out all the change when Rudy walks up and smiles.

"Red bean, Jimmy?"

"Yeah, and a side of hard cornbread," I answer.

Rudy reminds me of somebody but I don't know who. It's just a feeling, really, a familiar kind of gentleness that being such a rare quality makes you remember it, and those few who possess it somehow seem the same. I've also seen him break up a fight between a couple of horses who could've been bad guys on Wrestling, but he doesn't have a mean bone in his body.

He is the only restaurateur I know who has three different

grades of ice tea on the menu—Sweet, Not-So-Sweet and Unsweetened. Most folks who have been there have the Not-So-Sweet tea. Rudy's Sweet Tea is brewed with raw cane stalk and would send the uninitiated into a diabetic coma.

Rumor has it that some of the muckety-mucks from Coke came down one day just to have a taste and now only drink Coke for show at stockholder's meetings. Since I don't eat sweets it's my only vice.

I'm counting quarters and getting that first jolt from my tea when Rudy comes up and leans on the counter, watching me to try to figure out if what he's got to tell me is trouble or not.

"Ducky Nash was in here looking for you last week."

It's not a problem but it is a concern. Ducky is a... well, snitch is such an unkind-sounding word. Sort of like all those other tch words like witch and bitch. Even poor old Mrs. Fitch, who used to live across the way from us, and who accidentally sent Chester, her pet raccoon, through the spin cycle, prompting her to have nightmares so bad that she would sleepwalk out into her yard and sit in her car and honk the horn in the dead of night, seemed to have bad luck, though I don't know if it had anything to do with her name or not.

Let's just say that Ducky is an information broker.

I take another sip, nonchalantly, so that maybe Rudy will get up off his elbows. "Say what he wanted?"

Rudy raises up. "No. Just said it was important. Told him he could use the phone but he was acting all jumpy and beat it outta here."

I nod. "I'll try to catch up to him."

"That boy's all wrong, Jimmy. What you doing business with him for, not that it's any of my business."

"He just does odd jobs for me every once in awhile. For pocket money and such. You know how hard it is for these guys when they get out of the pokey. Besides, he keeps an eye out for my machines."

Rudy nods and turns away to fix my plate. He puts it down

in front of me and the smell alone is enough to feed the Five Thousand.

"Oh, by the way," he starts again, reaching under the counter.

I don't know if you've ever seen anyone make sausage or sling chitlins. I bring this up because to do it you start with a long, narrow skin, which in the case of sausage, for example, is attached to the meat grinder, and all the ground up sausage is sort of oozed into this skin until it stretches to what seems like the breaking point, and then it is tied off into a sausage. If you ever saw it you'd never forget it. And you probably wouldn't eat sausage for awhile either.

So when Rudy reaches down and pulls this thing from behind the counter and just thwacks it down right there in broad daylight, and me in the middle of my first mouthful of Nirvana, I think at first that it's one of these sausage/ chitlin skins. Until I realize that it's one of my Regulars, all mangled up and pitiful like some kid had found it in his Daddy's drawer, filled it with water, and chunked it off an overpass on I-85. All this takes about a half second, but I recoil and swallow my mouthful whole, which is a real tragedy.

"Good God," I said.

Rudy seems to take offense. "It's been laundered."

"I know, but Jesus, Rudy."

Rudy looks around just to show me that no one else is paying attention and then presses on.

"Grady Tutwiler gave it to me down at the barber shop. Said it blowed right out on him. Wanted to see if you'd make good on it."

I tried to work back to my Red Bean. "Sure. No problem."

"It ain't just the money," he explained. "I told you what his wife said to him. That seven children is enough for one lifetime and if he puts her in the family way again she's going to make absolute certain that it never happens again. If you take my meaning."

I reached into my satchel and sneaked a six-pack, covering it with my hand as I slid it across the counter.

"Here's half a dozen on the house."

Rudy smiled. "Grady'll appreciate that. He's one of your best customers. Says he don't mind paying full price if the service is good."

"Tell him thanks for me. And offer my apologies."

Rudy stuck the pack in his pocket and moved on down the counter. "Enjoy your lunch."

Which I did. Thoroughly. So thoroughly in fact that it made me want to go home and jump Charlotte in the shower. But I had business to attend to and Ducky Nash to worry about, and I'd be lying if the way he'd come in asking for me didn't make the hard cornbread lay a little heavy on my stomach.

Ducky's place was only a couple of streets over and a few blocks down. He lived in an old brick apartment house stuck near a drainage ditch where they'd built an offramp for the Expressway and figured that buying out the local gentry was too much trouble. Too many cars going overhead was the least of their worries. Most had lived in the same block since those apartments had been called flats. They had lived through flops and pads and cribs. Now they just called it run down.

I met Clarence 'Ducky' Nash about four years ago. He was severely pigeon-toed and when he got old enough to saunter it made him look like a duck in a hurry. I told him that the guy who used to do the voice of Donald Duck was named Clarence Nash and they called him Ducky too. Ducky didn't like that. Then I reminded him that if he hadn't learned to saunter people might have called him Pigeon Nash, and so he said it was fine by him if some other guy made funny noises for the cartoons and called himself Ducky Nash as long as he didn't do it around the guys in the neighborhood. I told him I thought that was a safe bet.

Ducky was what we in the industry refer to as a ghost.

Unless you were standing right there looking at him he simply did not exist. He'd never had a social security card, driver's license or voter registration card. He'd never registered for the draft, bought on credit or paid tax of any kind. He'd never had a job or done anything whatsoever that would have put him in anybody's computer system, or given him a single solitary number with which to identify him.

When I told him that was unusual, he was offended. When I found out he supported himself by petty burglaries, fencing a couple of televisions a week, I had him busted and sent to Granville for a couple of years where they gave him a whole slew of numbers.

He seemed to like that. And when he came out he became my eyes and ears in the neighborhood. He even showed me the social security card he'd gotten in prison. Said that since he was such a citizen now he might even get married.

Ducky lived in the back on the third floor. There wasn't an elevator and I dreaded the walk up. There were a thousand evil smells and together they made the smell of a thousand evils. It was a hodge-podge of spilled wine, spoiled food, garbage, urine, and the ancient mustiness of decaying wood. It was all like some eternal sadness heaving a slow sigh.

I made it to his floor only after accidentally stepping on the hand of an old lady who'd either been going up and had given up, or was going down and figured what's the hurry. She barely woke up, and even then just smiled at me before nodding off again. Her clothes reeked of mildew and wear.

Even before I knocked I smelled it. It was a smell I didn't recognize and that scared me. It was a potent smell, a thick, gooey smell that should have been accompanied by buzzing flies but wasn't. I had an idea what the smell was but didn't want to believe it.

The door was locked. I knocked quickly and loudly.

"Ducky? Ducky, you in there?"

I knew instinctively there wasn't going to be an answer and even as I called out again I was forcing the door. It wasn't hard. The old wood gave it up just as quickly as the people who lived there had.

It flung open and there was Ducky, sitting up in an old chair as if stuck there, his head hanging on his chest, his hands covering a huge knife wound in the belly. The blood was thick and hard and brown.

So I knew what the smell was but it didn't matter. Ducky was dead and whoever had done it hadn't been careful about it.

Then I got sick.

THREE

I hung around long enough to find out that Ducky had been dead for about three days and that bothered me. Ducky was always coming in and out of my life and almost always it was because he had some trouble. I didn't mind. He didn't seem to have anyone else.

But this was different. Coming into Rudy's all wired and asking for me only to end up dead very soon afterward made me feel that maybe I could've done something had I known.

My Grandmama, who fortunately passed away before her favorite grandson became a Revenooer, being as how she was known to do a little trading in the refreshment business herself once upon a time, used to say to me,

"Well, ignorance is bliss, now ain't it."

Only she would say it in a way with her lips squenched a little and in such a tone that let me know what she was really saying was exactly the opposite. That ignorance let people do hurtful things without so much as a conscience about it, and that wasn't right. She never said it in so many words, but I've always taken her meaning to be 'knowledge is responsibility'.

The more you know, the more you are required to do. And once you know something, then pleading ignorance later on down the line just makes it doubly wrong.

I took my last look at the worldly remains of Clarence 'Ducky' Nash and felt responsible.

I didn't want to stay long anyway, and it wasn't just the smell, the ungodly sight or the fact that I had gotten sick in the hall. All the cops were starting to give me the fisheye and I knew I had to hut it on out of there so that they could get on with it.

When the first cops arrived I flashed my badge, which I hardly ever do because I hate the looks I get. And sure enough, after giving the officer-in-charge my statement I saw a lot of noses start to wrinkle and I wasn't sure if it was the ambience or me.

Cops don't like me either, I'm sad to say. They don't like Feds in general, considering us kinda uppity and all, even if most of us are homegrown and maybe even grew up with some of them, but they all hate the I.R.S., and for the same reasons everyone else does, seeing as how we can get real personal and their badges won't help them like it would if they got caught fishing on private property or something and needed a little leeway.

I should tell you that it's not a geographical thing, and that on the whole the locals do a good job working with the Feds. Georgia is still, after all, a part of the Union and has been for the last hundred and twenty-five years this time around. And things really loosened up when we got one of our own elected to the White House back in '76, even if he did leave in disgrace and was replaced by a boy from California.

Besides, I've got a buddy from school who works for us up in Indiana and he says the locals treat him like pure-D trash. I guess we're just one of those things destined to be universally detested. Kind of like the New York Yankees.

But even the Big Whizzes of the local constabulary know better than to buck the Feds. That's a quick-fire way to have your hiney on Snuff Waldrep's Sunday menu. So when I ask to see a copy of the write-up when it's done before I beg my leave, they all nod.

Which brings me to why I'm driving the back way home with a hurt in my heart and a muddling in my brain.

I live in Decatur. Decatur used to be a town but now it's just a suburb of Atlanta. We used to have real honest-to-God neighborhoods with hundred year-old trees and churches and schools that had been there forever. Now we've got malls and strip shopping centers and fast-food restaurants and silly looking places where people can go to buy or do even sillier looking stuff, and the whole place looks like a back lot for bad T.V. movies.

I live in Old Decatur in an honest-to-God neighborhood, and in what I think is probably the world's largest garage apartment.

My landlady, Mrs. Bocook, is older than God and meaner than a snake, but with a good heart. She lives in one of those humongous white houses with massive columns on the porch like those they use the outside of in movies to make people believe that the grand indoors they've built in some warehouse in Hollywood is part of the same thing, and that only your upper-crust could live there. Well, it may be upper on the outside but it's all crust on the inside.

The inside of Mrs. Bocook's house looks like a flea market gone berserk. Every room and hallway in the entire house is stacked to the ceiling with junk. There's just a little trail blazed through or you couldn't get around at all, which gets narrower and narrower every year, but that's okay since Mrs. Bocook seems to be getting smaller, too. My first year there I spent a whole summer in a single room reading old newspapers. I spent a week just on Amelia Earhart.

The late Mr. Bocook, who they say died in the throes of desire on their fiftieth wedding anniversary, God keep him, had something like a black belt in carpentry. If the carpenters of the world had a secret handshake, he invented it.

When he retired he converted the old carriage house into a garage and workshop. After a few years Mrs. Bocook had that all cluttered up, so he added on, and added on. By 1970 he had over 2500 square feet and still didn't have room to fart, if you'll pardon the expression since Mrs. Bocook told me that herself. So he decided to build a second story. He had it all roughed in with plumbing and even a little kitchenette when his time came. Mrs. Bocook left it empty for awhile but then decided to rent it out. She said it was for the money, but since she never spends a nickel she doesn't have to, and seeing as how I sneaked a peek at her tax return once a few years back, I'm ashamed to say, and nearly had a heart attack, I think she did it because she wanted a little company.

Not that she'd ever let on. She's always on me to fix this or cut that or haul something off. But once when I'd had enough and told her I was thinking about finding another place to live, she got all red and told me that if I'd stay she'd leave me the garage in her will. She said she'd have to leave the main house to her son, who she doesn't seem to like very much ever since he ran off to Tuscon when he was sixty-five, but that's something else. So I stayed.

Of course I don't have a garage since you can't even stick your foot in longways without taking your life into your own hands, worrying that they'll find you some day under fifty years' worth of Redbooks, but I've decided not to do any building in Mrs. Bocook's lifetime. It just ain't worth the struggle.

Now I think the biggest reason Mrs. Bocook is so anxious for me to stay put is because of Charlotte, who has lived with me for the past three years, and who is the joy and sorrow of my life.

Maybe I should explain this.

When I was ten me and Petey Skinner went to the movies one Saturday when you could get in for six RC bottle caps and watch movies all day long. Usually Japanese monster movies. Now I wonder how they can make cars that run like Swiss watches, but back then couldn't make a King Kong that looked like a gorilla.

This particular day we decided to see who could eat the most JuJubes without getting sick. A couple thousand JuJubes later we were both pretty ripe, watching each other like two banty roosters. We spent the rest of the weekend together, not bathing or letting each other out of sight, even whizzing with the door cracked a little, which is rude and maybe even more than a little weird, but important to the seriousness of what we were doing. After two days we were both still holding them down and called it even.

Those damn JuJubes laid on my stomach a solid month, making it so that I couldn't breathe without my gut telling me that what I had done was unnatural. I couldn't stand the smell of food and couldn't look at a JuJube square on for nearly a year. I never got sick but my stomach was tender all the way into high school, and I couldn't stand the smell of anything sweet without burping, which made dating an adventure to say the least. Years later Petey got mustered out of the Navy a year early and I always thought it was the JuJubes.

From the first time I met Charlotte I've had that same feeling in my stomach. I can't stand to be without her for more than twelve hours at a time. She went to visit her sister once and I got the cold sweats in the middle of the night and drove down below Macon and rented a motel room just so I could watch the house, knowing that she was sleeping inside, until a cop came along and asked me was I a sicko or just lost.

If anything ever happened to us I'd call in sick and then just shoot myself.

People used to think that Charlotte was slow. Her Mama ran off with a Pentecostal evangelist out of Valdosta who was having a tent meeting that summer, and her Daddy never talked to her. So she never talked to anybody. She still doesn't talk much but she's not slow.

Two years ago we went on vacation up in Charleston, West Virginia, because they built a dog-racing track up there. We were walking along the arena where they parade the dogs just before they race and Charlotte was all serious, stooping down and craning her neck and studying each dog for a solid minute each time, making little marks in her program. She did this before every race and by the sixth race had picked three winners, one second and only one that finished out of the money, mainly because he tripped and got run over by all the other dogs.

Charlotte was ahead by over two hundred dollars and so I asked her what was she looking at. She got a little flustered and bashful and I was about to drop it when she pulled me off to the side.

"It's their dooleys, Jimmy," she whispered.

"Ma'am?"

"Their dooleys. See, you got big dogs with big ones and you gotta figure they know this and got no heart for when the chips are down. Then you got littler dogs with big ones and you gotta figure they got nothing else to prove.

But you take your big dogs with little ones...you know they know they've been shortchanged and ain't about to let it go."

I boosted our bets to the fifty dollar window. Before the weekend was out we were up over three thousand dollars. We would have stayed longer except that Charlotte was afraid the sickness would get us, and she was probably right. We took our winnings and drove over to Pigeon Forge and lived the good life for the rest of the week. Charlotte has a rainy-day bank and we have a custom of putting a quarter in it every time we make love. By the time we left Pigeon Forge we had spent most of our winnings but the bank had grown by over six dollars.

Charlotte is also the only natural blonde I've ever known who bleaches her hair. During the winter her hair is the color of cream candy but during the summer the sun turns it white. And naturally her roots are darker. So she bleaches her roots to keep people from thinking she's a bottle blonde. She's funny that way.

She used to wait tables at a sports bar and I used to go in there to try to put in some machines. It wasn't long before I would go in there when she first came on her shift and there wasn't a crowd just so we could talk. I never was much of a drinker and it was making my stomach hurt all the time. Finally I had to tell her I couldn't come in for awhile.

"Why not?"

"Well, because I'm not really a drinker."

"Then you shouldn't hang out in bars so much."

"I know. But up until now the heartache of not seeing you was worse than the bellyache of drinking so much beer."

We had our first kiss right then and there. Our first date was sort of anticlimactic.

I've only hit one person in anger my entire life, even after nine years as a Fed. That was Paul Doody, and with a handle like that you know I hated to do it, but he took the mouthpiece off my trombone in eighth grade band and put it down his pants before putting it back. People started snickering when I started playing, which wasn't that unusual in itself except that now it was people who couldn't even hear me from where they were, and somebody finally told me what he'd done. So I clocked him a good one. At our tenth year reunion somebody told me that he'd joined The Moonies and I wondered if I had anything to do with it.

I came close again one night when I came into the bar to see Charlotte. It was Super Bowl Sunday and people were rowdy. One guy in there was so loud and obnoxious and stupid-looking that I knew right off he'd gone to Georgia. He had three buddies and they were guffawing and carrying on in a way that made me understand why people in Hollywood seem to think we're all like that, and then he made his first mistake.

Something got spilled and he called Charlotte stupid, and he did it loud enough for people to hear, and he did it so that his buddies would think he was the Spring Bull.

I got up and Charlotte gave me a look like she didn't want me to get all bruised on her account. I was holding my temper the best I could and walked over to the table. I told the guy that I was a friend of the lady's and knew firsthand that she wasn't stupid. Furthermore, I informed him that it was his own ample midsection, which was uncovered between his T-shirt and pants in a way that made his belly button look like a blimp-eye-view of Fulton County Stadium, that had jostled the table and spilled his beer. He snorted like an old hog and gave his buddies the eye.

He stood up and that was his second mistake. I moved in belt-to-belt, which still nearly put me out of striking range, and asked him to step outside. He did and his buddies came with him. He could tell I was serious and that made him nervous because he kept looking at his buddies with a twitch in his eye, but they were all grinning and egging him on. I politely asked them to go back inside since this was between him and me.

When they laughed I flashed my badge, which I hate to do but there you have it, and told them that if they didn't move it inside right quick I'd not only have them audited for the last four generations, but would have all their in-laws audited, too, and make sure they all knew whose fault it was. They looked like ants who'd just had their hill peed on by a dog.

I could see all the fight go out of him once his friends were gone. I still wanted to give him a good pounding but I heard Grandmama's voice in my head. That here was a man who'd never had much power of his own. Maybe his Daddy had whipped him too much and his wife treated him like a bug. I also knew just how much I loved Charlotte and that scared the Hell out of me. He promised to apologize to her and that was the end of it.

Except I didn't go back in right away. I was all torn up and didn't know why. After a few minutes Charlotte came out looking for me. I was almost bawling by then, but I had to tell her that I wasn't just an honest rubber man but a Fed, and a demon Revenooer to boot.

You know what she told me? That she had known there was something special about me right off, and that she had wanted to tell me so but didn't know how. She had this proud look on her face that would have lasted the rest of my life even if I hadn't seen it since, which I have.

I did cry a little then, but got over it quick when she moved in with me the next weekend. She is a floral designer now and has a gift for it. She's even talking about going freelance, but would need some place to work. I told her to forget about building on as long as Mrs. Bocook's alive, so she's looking into renting a little shop somewhere.

Charlotte gets a lot of smelly chemicals on her hands from handling dried flowers and she's insecure about it. She won't come near me until she's tended to them and goes through a family-size bottle of hand lotion every two days. She smells like a hospital nursery during visiting hours but I like it.

She asked me to marry her a couple of weeks ago. It was Petey and the JuJubes all over again. She said that she wanted us to have a baby and that she wanted it all to be above board. We compromised. I told her that if she got pregnant we'd get married and so we stopped taking precautions.

We've averaged trying twice a day for the past couple of weeks, even though we both know that there's only two days the entire month she can conceive and that won't start until next week sometime. We don't mind.

I pull into the driveway and park near the outside stairway to the loft, which is what Charlotte calls it and got me in the habit. I stay clear of the garage ever since a jet taking off from Hartsfield International set off a rumble that caused a mountain of Christmas ornaments to avalanche onto my van. I'm so upset that I don't see there's a couple of those fat cherub bulbs on my antenna until I pull up to work the next day and my boss sees them and asks me if I'm trying to be cute. I shake my head, thinking that if I was trying to be cute I'd have said that I was building his family tree as a hobby.

Charlotte's in the yard with Mrs. Bocook. Mrs. Bocook's doing all the talking with one of those baskets she heisted from Winn-Dixie hanging on her arm like an over-sized purse. She's dipping into it every so often and shaking a handful of brown stuff around her azalea bushes. Charlotte is following around behind her, watching her intently, listening as if every word was the God's honest truth, which is the real way to Mrs. Bocook's heart.

"Some people claim that cow shit or pig shit is the best, but they don't know what they're talking about," she's saying.

And right away I know that I don't want any part of it. Except that Charlotte sees me and waves me over. Mrs. Bocook doesn't seem to notice and goes right on.

"None of that chemical pooey, either. It's fish guts and

chicken shit. That's what makes these babies bloom. The hard part is to get the mixture just right so that the smell won't kill you. You use topsoil for that. You set your fish guts and your chicken shit out to dry on something metal, a piece of aluminum siding works good because it gets hot enough to keep the critters away but not so hot that the smell makes your neighbors call the law on you. Then you mix that up good, and add three parts topsoil. Then you got fertilizer worth braggin' about."

"Yes, Ma'am," Charlotte says.

Then Mrs. Bocook sees that she's lost her audience and sees me coming across the yard, and scowls at me.

"Oh," she says. "It's him."

I give Charlotte a little peck on the cheek but stay out of arm's reach because I don't know if her hand has been in the basket or not. Mrs. Bocook ignores me and continues to layer on her concoction.

"Charlotte's got a knack with green things," she says. "Needs to know what's what."

"Yes, Ma'am," I answer.

"You get another cat, Jimmy?" she asks after a second.

"No, Ma'am. Why?"

She turns and grins at me before moving off to the next clump of bushes. "Just wonderin' what's been making that God-awful yowlin' of a night."

Charlotte just looks at me and smiles. She seems to know that something's wrong because she always sticks her hand in my hip pocket, which I would enjoy even if something was wrong, when she thinks something's wrong.

No sooner do we get upstairs than she asks me.

"Something happen on your route today?"

She always refers to my job as my route, as if that was all that needed to be said.

So I told her. I told her all about Ducky and how he had been looking for me and how he had done something to get himself killed and how I knew I had to do something about it, but didn't know what.

"You'll find out," she says, helping me off with my shirt. "And when you do you'll feel better."

"I hope so," I say.

About four times during the three years we've been living together something has gotten to me so bad that it shows. The last time was when there was a big hubbub over the budget and they threatened to transfer me to Columbia, South Carolina, which I'm sure is a very nice place and maybe even one Hell of a condom market, but which may as well be Juneau, Alaska to somebody who loves where he is and doesn't want to go anywhere. And all four times Charlotte has done something that I don't understand, and think that maybe that's my true quest in life. To figure it out.

She fixes my supper and it's always one of my favorites.

She tells me the story of something we've shared, and in tones so gentle and low and filled with love that it sounds like an angel speaking through a dream.

She runs me a bath and puts a little lotion in the water.

She washes my hair and makes sure none of the suds gets in my eyes.

She takes me to bed.

Then holds me until I fall asleep.

And that is why she is the joy and sorrow of my life.

FOUR

I don't really know how it happened, but I've got a suspicion that when all the High Poobahs of the days of yore were sitting around discussing what type of buildings they would build to house all the Government offices, they decided to build things that folks would recognize in no uncertain terms, and for as long as it took the bulk of the population to learn to read.

It does have its advantages, though. I hardly ever get lost on the way to work any more and it put Ducky's parole officer close by.

I was dreading talking to him for a couple of reasons. First, I had to be mindful of my cover, which wasn't that big a problem as long as I dressed like a Fed and didn't offer him any free samples. Besides, there are scuds of Feds running around this part of Geogia, the exact number of which I ain't saying on account of it would only make you mad.

The second was that Ducky's parole officer was Lee Sharpley, and he got on my nerves. I've known Lee a long time from a distance but have only spoken to him twice. He is what some of the less generous among us refer to as an Uncle Tim. That's somebody from here who goes off to some big Yankee school, living the high life with guys named Brent and Lance, and then comes back to show us once and for all just how utterly ignorant we are.

Lee wears penny loafers and argyle socks. Puh-lease, and pass the Pepto.

You have to believe that he did it on purpose, too. To prove that, yes, he had been away and only came back to this lowly place out of pity. All the Republicans loved it, but to most of the hard-working stiffs around here it went over like Jane Fonda at a D.A.R. soiree.

I got shown right in and there was Lee talking on the phone, purring into it like a milk-fed cat, his feet propped up on his desk, showing—you guessed it, tan penny loafers and a pair of brown socks with green and gold triangles.

I don't want you to think that I've got some kind of foot fetish, but it did bring back some bad memories of Al 'my pal' Katz. Al is a big-time tax lawyer in town who calls everybody 'Pal'. Of course Al really is a Yankee, coming down here to carpetbag a tad, and he wears loafers, too, the kind with a tassel on the front, but doesn't wear any socks at all. He's arrogant about it, too. He holds court in his office not wearing any socks and I heard that he even went to a tax hearing that way once until the judge asked,

"Somebody's wallet get wet?"

Al's big because he finds all the loopholes and manufactures others. He always blusters a lot when his client's in a jam and you'd be surprised just how effective that can be because around here a yawn is about as demonstrative as most people get. I begrudge no man earning a living even if he has to be aggressive, but at the first hint of impropriety Al's outta there like a possum on the highway, leaving his client holding the bag, and that's pretty poor if you ask me.

Al used to have a habit of meeting all the new agents every year, just to show that we're all professionals and on the up-and-up, even if some of us are more up-and-up than others. Some he takes to lunch at the Ritz. Me he took to a Braves game.

This was a few years back when the Braves were such an embarrassment that you could buy a ticket in the nosebleed seats and by the third inning move on up to the second row. Hell, by the fifth inning you could sit in Ted Turner's box.

We went to this game and Al talks the whole time. I swear to God, which I don't like to do but wanted you to take this seriously, his mouth is relentless. People are even moving because of it but Al just keeps on jawing. Finally, along about the seventh inning some big stumper with work boots and a Red Man cap sitting behind us has had enough and tells Al that if he doesn't shut his flap in a skinny minute he's going to make a very sensitive part of his anatomy much larger than what the Good Lord intended, the means of which I ain't saying. Al clams up like an errant husband and I start believing in Cosmic Justice again.

After the game I follow this guy out at a discreet distance so that I can get the tag number off his truck. When I get back to the office I track him down, pull his file and put an official 'Do Not Audit' tag on it for an indefinite period of time, just so he can sleep easy for awhile even if he doesn't know why. I also have six of Al's biggest clients audited as a matter of principle and we don't hear a peep out of him again.

Lee smiles and points to a chair and I sit. He hangs up and we shake.

"Jim," he says. He calls me Jim to let me know that I'm no big potato. "What can I do for you?"

"I understand you're Clarence Nash's parole officer."

"Ducky?" he says, grinning in a way that's not the least bit respectful. "What's your interest in Ducky?"

"He did odd jobs for me now and then. He was supposed to do something for me over the weekend and when he didn't show, I went to see what was what."

"And the 'what' was that he had bought it."

"Yeah. I found him."

This seems to make Lee a little more serious, if not respectful. He reaches into a drawer and pulls out a file.

"He showed up on time. Never got busted again. No trouble that I know of."

"So you don't have any idea why somebody would want to kill him?"

He waves his hand in dismissal and I'm surprised when I don't see a pinky ring.

"Street stuff. You know, law of the jungle and all that. Half these guys wind up dead before forty. They can't seem to avoid it. It's a shame, but..." And he waves his hand again.

"You looking into it?" I ask, watching him just to let him know that I know what his answer is going to be before he says it, and that it's ten-to-one he won't look me in the eye when he says it.

He bites. "Nothing to look into. I've got fifty guys just like him and the only thing they've got going for them is that they're still alive."

I sit for a minute just because I know it makes him uncomfortable. I don't do much for spite ever, but I want him to know that I know he just doesn't give a doo, and that there is at least one person in this world who won't pat him on the back and tell him it's alright and then set a tee time for next Tuesday. I stand to leave. This time we nod but don't shake.

I'm almost to the foyer when I see Dumb Eddie and Slick pull up outside in a City Delivery van and that seems odd since neither of them has ever done anything more legitimate than what they're doing right now, which is putting a quarter into the parking meter. I duck behind a column. They know who I am and it's not as a Fed.

It's not hard to see them. Dumb Eddie is six-four and over three hundred pounds. Slick is, well, slick. But more important is that he never goes anywhere without Dumb Eddie.

Eddie's a four-time loser who specializes in being the world's worst burglar. Every time he's been busted it's for doing something stupid. One time he set off the alarm breaking into a K-Mart and when the cops came he tried to escape in a go-cart. They found him pushing it down Peachtree when he ran out of gas.

Everyone knows that Slick is the real criminal and that Eddie just drives and crashes in an occasional door, but Slick always manages to stay out of the slammer.

I feel sorry for Dumb Eddie. I think they call him that just because all the other Eddie nicknames have been taken. I don't know first-hand that he's really all that dumb, but hanging out with Slick would qualify.

Slick doesn't care if there have been beaucoups other guys named Slick. They don't call him that because of how he looks or how he acts. In fact, he's always kind of scummy, usually dressed in old jeans and a T-shirt, and his hair has so many cowlicks in it that he gave it up a long time ago.

They call him Slick because his hands sweat so bad that nobody can get a decent print, and that's the truth. He got popped for a drug store break-in once and sure enough they couldn't get a matching print and he just slithered away.

Seeing them in that van bothered me. There wasn't anything that unusual about Dumb Eddie checking in with his own parole officer, seeing as how he got sprung again not too long ago, and having Slick along was just his way of doing things. But something started a little nagging tug in my gut. It was only a two on the Petey-JuJube scale but it wouldn't let me go.

I finished my route in a hurry, which I am loathe to do since it cuts way down on my visiting. Then I decide to try to catch up to Slick and Dumb Eddie.

To accomplish this I utilize all my training and investigative skills. I call the dispatcher at City Delivery and tell her that I just got visited by a boy the size of Virginia who left somebody else's package at my place of business, and how might I catch up to him. She tells me that she'll be happy to have him swing back by and I tell her I'm on my way out.

So that is how I came to be sitting in the parking lot of the Siemens plant. Sure enough, Dumb Eddie is making a delivery and Slick is riding shotgun. I don't know if he is an employee or just along for the scenery, but I do stop to wonder if maybe having a big company around with the name of Siemens and just letting it go by is one of the reasons this country is in the shape it's in.

I follow Dumb Eddie around for the rest of the day and all he does is make deliveries. He isn't in any kind of hurry and it's not hard to keep up. They were still on the road at six and stopped for supper. So I took advantage of the time and called Charlotte to tell her I'd be late. I've never talked to her on the phone when she didn't make me glad to be young and alive.

"I was thinking that maybe you was mad at me because we didn't do nothing last night," she says, "so I went out and bought me a new nightie."

She breaks my heart into a jillion pieces and it takes a second to catch my breath.

"You take too good care of me, Sweetheart," I said. "And I could never be mad at you."

"What about the time I accidentally got my special undies mixed up with yours in the washer and you had to wear pink drawers to work?"

"It didn't matter. Nobody saw them."

"You cussed. Loud, too, as I recall."

"But not at you. Just in general."

"Oh. Just checking."

"Well I'll be home as quick as I can."

"I got veal cutlets for supper," she says, which is her way of telling me that I'm going to need all the iron I can get in my system for later on. My throat gets a little thick.

"Love you," I whisper.

"Jesus, Jimmy," she purrs and giggles at the same time, how I don't know. "I know that."

It's nearly seven when Eddie hits the Interstate and points the truck toward Tucker, which I know to mean that they are calling it a day since that's where the main terminal is. I decide to stick with them just because I don't like loose ends.

If Decatur used to be a neighborhood then Tucker used to be the boonies. Only they didn't carve out their version of The American Dream out of what used to be a town, but out of pine trees. They left a goodly amount of woods here and there, sometimes with a clump stuck right out in the middle of a driveway. I guess they wanted to convince themselves that they hadn't really taken all that much advantage of Mother Nature after all, but with all the industrial parks and office complexes around it looks like something Walt Disney would have done if he'd been a redneck.

The City Delivery terminal was in a part that's still surrounded by boonies, tucked back in the trees far enough to keep wayward Yankee tourists from mistaking it for a Hardee's, and with its own road. It posed a little bit of a problem for me, though, since there was no way for me to follow them in without being seen. I was in my van with Piedmont Specialties painted on the side, and so I finally decided the best approach was to cruise on in like I didn't have good sense. If I got stopped I could always ask for a cheeseburger.

It was nearly eight o'clock but still light out since Daylight Savings Time kicked in a couple of weeks back. There weren't many people about and almost all the trucks and vans were parked and locked up for the night.

Eddie parked his at the far end and I laid back a good ways, concealed between a couple of big Step-Vans. Slick got out and moved off to the employee parking area where there were only two cars left. One was a new Olds Ninety Eight and the other was a rusted out Gremlin that had once been purple, which not only isn't made any more, but which the entire company is merely vapors. No prizes for guessing which car was Slick's.

Then I'm thinking I'm wrong as Slick walks over to the Ninety-Eight. He gets there and the passenger window comes down and he sticks his head in. I see him take something— it could be a note, it could be a cigarette or it could be all the secret passwords for the Strategic Air Command. Or it could even be one of my lilac Ribbed, which is a real up-and-comer in the trade—and put it in his shirt pocket. After a minute he and Dumb Eddie get into the Gremlin and rumble off.

I hunch down and they don't so much as glance in my direction as they drive away. I feel a little stupid, I admit. On television you can pull right across the street and the suspected evildoer can come out of his house, take a good look around, then get in his car and drive away without even seeing you. I was a good hundred yards away and felt utterly naked. The only thing going for me was that my van was the same color as all the others–white–and that being scrunched in between two trucks made it nearly impossible to read my logo on the side.

It must have worked because the driver of the Olds doesn't see me either. Which is a good thing since I sat up so fast that I accidentally tooted the horn, and bumped my knee on the steering column so hard that I hollered out an ugly word so loud that it could be heard out back of Cartersville. And the Petey-JuJube scale jumped to a good seven-and-a-half.

The guy driving the car was Lee Sharpley.

FIVE

I have a gun. I have to, it's part of my job. Mine's a .32 I keep in a lockbox welded to the floor of my van during the day and in my underwear drawer at night. I never shoot it and wouldn't even load it if I didn't think people would find out and start calling me Barney Fife.

I hate guns. I hate all guns, but especially handguns. You see kids turn up dead because what to us was cap pistols and Cowboys & Indians is the real thing to them and they play for keeps.

Now I don't know for sure, but I suspect that once a long, long time ago a bunch of the Grand Wasirs of law enforcement got together and decided that guns were a deterrent, mainly because they had liked Cowboys & Indians as kids and hadn't gotten over it. That's what they call guns even today. A deterrent.

The only problem is that it's not a deterrent. In the first place the only way a gun would be a deterrent is if you used it on somebody, and then it didn't really work as much of a deterrent, now did it? And in the second place the bad guys use them, too, I guess as sort of anti-deterrents, and are probably more disposed to do so, and then you've got a mess on your hands.

The fear of being dead doesn't seem to be much of a deterrent, either, since most of the bad guys grew up the hard way and don't cherish life or they wouldn't have guns in the first place. And the fear of the pokey is not what it used to be because everybody eats good and they've got cable.

Now a big stick's a deterrent. That's what I've always admired about the British because their cops use big sticks.

See, you take your average criminal and he knows that if he gets caught he's going to get whomped with a big stick, then some of the edge is taken off of even eating good and having cable. Who could stomach Jethro Bodine with a knot on their noggin?

Sticks aren't much good for distance, either. So it doesn't matter if the bad guys have anti-deterrent sticks. Unless they can chuck it with great accuracy a stick isn't going to help a whole lot. All the cop has to do is chase him up a tree and wait for other cops, and the criminal knows that if he doesn't drop his stick real polite like, he's going to get walloped. So that's why I think we ought to take away everybody's guns and give them sticks.

Either that or keep all the guns so the gun companies won't suffer, and rig them to only shoot soap bubbles.

It would make it safer in the woods, too. I've got an uncle that's been shot four times. He has a gift for making realistic gobbler sounds and it has become his life's work. He carves these little do-hickeys that he jams into his mouth and yodels, which is harder than it sounds, and gobblers fly right up and proposition him. The only problem is that he's gotten so good at it hunters mistake him for the real thing and shoot at him. The last time he got blown right out of a tree and broke his leg in three places. So he gave it up and took up cross stitch.

His house is full of turkey doilies.

Another reason I guess I feel this way about guns is because every six months I have to re-qualify with my weapon and it's a tragedy. One time I scored six out of eight only to find out that it was on the third target over. When I come to the range the instructors match pennies to see who gets the honors. And they all wear steel-toed shoes on account of a little accident I had a couple of years back, which I swear wasn't my fault. How was I supposed to know that twirling it a few times before holstering it wasn't standard operating procedure.

So that's why I'm driving north to the old homestead where I can shoot my gun without fear of injuring anybody. I'm also a little depressed, which I hardly ever am, but I need to get away from town for a day. I read Ducky's obituary in the paper this morning and it was only three lines. I call the mortuary to inquire about services and it only gets worse. They tell me that since Ducky's indigent, which is what they call people when they're down and out, it's a freebie on the County and they're going to cremate him. They also ask me if I want the urn when they're done.

"Surely he's got some family or something," I say.

The man sounds so sincere that I wonder if he couldn't make a better living selling cars.

"It's a lovely urn. Quite decorative. You could put it on the mantelpiece and no one would ever question that it wasn't there for art's sake."

"I'll think about it."

"Well, you've got thirty days, Bud. After that we park him at Potter's with all the other deadbeats."

Then he hangs up on me. And I wonder if we all haven't lost something that used to sustain us. That if we haven't become so self-sufficient we forget we couldn't survive in this world without other people.

Me, I've got my own problems.

My folks live on the same two hundred acres that have been in the family since before the war, by which I mean the War Between the States, the only one that mattered. It's mostly rolling hill and rock, but over the years they've cleared enough to have the makings of a pretty decent farm, except that it was never used for that. They've had gardens and livestock, but when Monroe had the double-wide put in part of the deal was that the pigs had to go, since it wasn't respectable. So now there's just a little vegetable patch and some chickens.

Daddy cut timber and had his own little sawmill. I used to tell people that until I got into college and they told me I sounded just like John-Boy Walton and was I using that as a way to meet girls.

I don't think people realize just how mountainous parts of

Georgia are. But once you get above Atlanta you're in the Smokies and can't go far without seeing somebody you probably saw in *Deliverance.*

The day is warm and the drive is nice and I get there in one piece. I would've brought Charlotte except that this is a work day and besides, I don't like the way Monroe looks at her. I pull up and my stomach does a little flop because sure enough, there's Monroe's truck. He's got a big red GMC with so many gadgets that it looks like he's the Grand Marshal of the Shriner's Parade.

I'm not driving my van today. Even my folks don't know exactly what I do. I'm not sure they'd understand what a condom is anyway and no way am I going to explain it to them. Instead I'm driving Mrs. Bocook's Nash, which is over thirty years old and has less than nine thousand original miles on it. She hates to drive and gets around by mooching off some of her old biddy friends, which is not as unChristian as it sounds should you happen to meet any of them. And every once in awhile she accosts me and tells me to take the Nash out for a stretch.

I no sooner walk in the door when I see Mama standing in the living room all aglow like she's just had a vision and stroking a brand new VCR like it's an old coon dog that just came in off a three-week prowl. Monroe's sitting in the big chair grinning to himself, which is his way of giving it to me.

"Oh look, Jimmy," she says so sweet. "See what Monroe has brung us?"

I force a smile and then say to Monroe, "So where's your tape?" which is my way of giving it back to him.

Daddy and I head toward the woods in back of the house while Mama starts fixing something to eat. Monroe wants to come along but Daddy won't allow it, which is his way of not playing favorites, except that if the whole truth be known I've got to believe that having a boy as terrible with a firearm as I am is the sorrow of his life. Being a Fed, he can tolerate. Being a Revenooer, he can stomach. But hating guns, well that's downright unnatural.

He takes my gun and checks it out.

"I don't know why you're afraid of this little thing, Jimmy. It'd take two or three good shots to kill somebody unless you hit 'em just right."

"I'm not afraid of it, Daddy. I just don't like it."

He points to a knothole in a pine tree about fifty feet away. He aims and pulls off four quick shots, all of which hit the knothole. Then he hands the gun to me.

I take aim and fire a single shot. I have to study for a second to see where it went, but then I see that I'm about eighteen inches high and six inches to the right.

"You hit the tree leastways," Daddy says.

I take aim again and that's when Daddy steps up.

"Forget about all that cockamamie stuff they showed you in boot camp."

"Training Academy."

"Here. Don't sight with one eye like that. That's best left for rifles when you got your cheek on the same line. Close your left eye." I do. "Now close your right eye." I do. "What happens?"

"I can't see anything. My eyes are closed."

Daddy grunts low in his throat, which is his way of telling me I'm trying his patience.

"Do 'em one-at-a-time," he grumbles. I do. "What happens?"

"It moves," I said, which it does.

"That's what I mean. You can't sight that way. Now keep both eyes open. And look straight down over top of the sight."

"There's two of 'em," I said, which there were.

Daddy shakes his head like he's going to whack me one. "Then stick the knuckle of your damn thumb up there and sight with that."

I do and take aim. I fire and see dirt fly up at the foot of the tree.

"Horseshit. You dipped it."

"I did that because I always seem to shoot high and wanted to compensate."

"You did that because you let the gun get away from you and the shot throws the barrel up. That's kid stuff, Jimmy."

"Yes, sir," and my voice is about twelve years old.

He grabs me and holds me firm. "Now keep it on line. Don't let it move an inch. Hold it like you got good sense. FIRE!"

I do but hear the bullet as it tears through the branches high overhead.

"Great God Almighty!" Daddy bellows. "I believe you shanked a crow."

"You made me jump," I protest, and I must admit that my head's sagging a little.

"Ah, you never was much good in the woods. Not like Monroe."

I hate it when this happens. So I take aim and do it my way. Relax, sight, breathe.

"You mean like the time you and Monroe went squirrel hunting and Monroe tears off after an albino squirrel?"

"Well..." Daddy says sheepishly.

I fire. A good hit.

"Mama almost made him eat that cat."

Daddy goes quiet and I go through it all again. Relax, sight, breathe.

"Or the time you and Monroe are frog giggin' and Monroe hollers that he sees a red-eyed frog and chunks the gig before you can tell him there ain't such a thing?"

"Well..."

I fire again. Another good hit.

"It took all you had to outrun that snake."

I lower my gun and look at him. He grins real big and puts his arm around my shoulder.

"I think you've got the hang of it, Son."

We're all sitting at the table. We've got fried chicken, some fresh succotash, rice and chicken gravy, and some of Mama's coffee can biscuits, named that because she uses a coffee can to shape the biscuit from the sheet of dough, which makes them extra-large I admit, but Monroe can eat one in two bites, one if it's his first bite of the meal.

We drink ice tea out of these glasses that hold about a quart which Mama got two summers ago at the Hess station, and which she always breaks out when Monroe's there because they look dressy.

Monroe eats like the stud lab rat. I hate to watch because I think that maybe someday I'll lose an eye from the sparks off his knife and fork. Also, because it makes me wonder if he isn't in training to go tag-team with my boss at Wrestle Mania XXXVIII.

I take after Daddy. He eats slow and never says a word. Mama hardly ever eats while we're at the table. She nibbles and watches us and occasionally tries to stir up the conversation.

"Monroe was just telling me about a new business deal," she says.

"Oh yeah?" I reply.

Monroe doesn't say anything. He's afraid of breaking his rhythm.

"What is it?" I ask, if only to keep Mama from staring at me.

"Indoor golf," he says, except that with his mouth so full it sounds like 'woody biff'.

Mama sees fit to jab him one in the arm and he takes a breather.

"You mean miniature golf?" I ask.

He shakes his head and stifles a burp. "Regular golf. Except that it's all indoors."

I am speechless. "You mean put a roof over a golf course?"

"Yeah. Except that it wouldn't be a whole golf course. Just two holes, a par three and a par five which could be a par four. All the tees and traps are portable so that it could be changed around and you'd get the same feel as if you were playing a bunch a different holes."

"With a roof over it."

"Yeah, it'd have to be a big 'un, too."

"And how much is it going to cost to do that?"

He shrugs. "Ten, twelve million dollars."

I get part of a biscuit hung, thinking that somebody has spent some time with Monroe and thinks that here is a long-term vacation opportunity way down South somewhere, like Brazil.

"Wouldn't that be a little boring?" I ask innocently. "To walk back and forth between two holes?"

Monroe stares at me like I just told him the hunting dog he paid eight hundred dollars for has some poodle in it.

I continue as tactfully as I can. "And you'd have people standing in line for hours just to play. There'd be no way to keep them occupied. And how would you know who's on what hole so that you could make the adjustments? And making them for every player would just slow things down even more."

Monroe digs in again, which is his way of reclaiming life from the jaws of misfortune.

"It's just an idea," he says, which comes out 'boo de bee be-un'.

"Yeah," I say sympathetically. "The taxes would probably kill you anyway."

The fork starts to fly at Mach 2 and Mama looks at me like I've hurt Monroe's feelings on purpose. Daddy just stares off as if the outside world is a Hell of a lot more interesting, or else he's about to bust a gut and doesn't want to let on.

Then I see the same look in Monroe's eyes I saw the day they turned him loose on Joe Montana three downs in a row, which rumor has it that the last time they bend down to ask Joe where he is he says 'DisneyWorld'.

And I see that he's fixed on the chicken plate, which as it happens is occupied by a single piece. He smirks at me and stabs out so quick that I think he's been taking lessons from Mr. Wu and Mr. Wu's Full-Service Laundry and Karate Academy.

He takes a big bite in my general direction, enjoying every chew and slurping his fingers.

"Don't count that chicken 'til your fingers need lickin'," he says, which is his way of giving me the 'same to you'.

"That's okay," I say sweetly. "I hear Mama say that the next time we're up she's going to fix albino squirrel."

SIX

I go in to work especially early the next morning to do some snooping before anybody else gets there. And nobody is except for Mrs. Monahan, our cleaning lady. She's in my boss's office with arms flying, wearing heavy rubber gloves and a mask that makes her look like she's getting ready to take somebody's appendix out, which I'm sure she'd do to my boss if she had the chance.

I stick my head in to speak. "Throws up a lot of dust, does he?"

She looks at me in a way that tells me that we both know that every speck of dust within three counties sticks to him like glue on account of he's so wet all the time.

"It ain't the dust," she says. "it's the stink."

I don't know what to say to that so I just nod as my way of commiserating.

"He works hard," I say finally.

"The man's a pig," she answers, and then shoos me away because she's getting ready to break out the heavy artillery, which is a can of industrial strength Lysol.

I'm pooped already. I know you're probably thinking that this has something to do with Charlotte, and it does, only not in the way you're probably thinking.

Just before we drift off last night she says she finally figured out who it is I remind her of.

"Who's that?" I ask.

"That boy who played on 'My Three Sons'."

This wounds me and it's hard to hide it. "But I don't wear glasses."

"No, Jimmy. Not the weenie-one with the buck teeth. The

oldest one."

"You mean the boy who played in 'Spin & Marty' on the old 'Mickey Mouse Club'?"

"No, not that oldest one. The oldest one when they started doing it in color instead of black & white."

"Oh," I say. "That's very sweet, Honey."

And before you know it we had another quarter in the kitty.

But that's not why I'm tired. I'm tired because I don't know what I'm doing. People rarely die in Revenue investigations unless they decide it just ain't worth it and jump in front of a MARTA bus, which are painted in the national colors of Luxembourg, but that's a different story.

I decide my first choice is to do what I normally do, which is to pull up files on the computer and stare at them until something clicks in my head. Something always does. Don't ask me how I do this because I don't know. I had a guy with the Justice Department tell me one time that it was downright scary. But you shouldn't be scared. Even if you live in my jurisdiction. I just want to give you a gentle reminder that I went to college and ain't as dumb as I look.

I pull up the quarterly payroll records for City Delivery. They list the amount of tax withheld from each of their employees. This lets me know who's doing well, who's doing middlin' and who they might have parted company with recently.

The first thing that catches my eye is that they've got a guy on the payroll who I know to be an ex-con. Now this in itself is not a crime, and in fact could be considered progressive and charitable, and rightly so. Maybe one of the higher-ups had a favorite uncle who strayed from the path a time or two and this was his way of doing his part.

But this guy was sent up for manslaughter and must've had this job waiting for him. I can't tell if Slick is on the payroll because I don't know his real name.

I do find out that Dumb Eddie's real name is Edwin and I have to admit I was embarrassed for him.

Then I see something that hurts me quick and hurts me bad.

Like the time back when we were kids and Monroe and I were playing Little League. Naturally we were on opposing teams. Even then we both seemed to know that neither of us had a future in baseball, but Monroe had something most other kids didn't, other than a sixteen-inch neck. And that was a curveball.

It was a thing of sheer glory, too. He'd start that sucker about head high and all the other kids would duck, while the ball started to break just as pretty as you please until it landed in the catcher's mitt like a butterfly on a fence post. And also right in the middle of the strike zone.

I knew this and was determined not to budge. In the semi-final round of the league championship that year I stood in the batter's box with Monroe giving me the bird dog and I knew *The Swoop*, which was what he called it, was coming. So I waited it out and when it broke I poked it over the left field fence.

The next time I came up with the game on the line. And sure enough, Monroe gave me that same look. So I waited. Only this time he didn't throw *The Swoop* and the ball hit me flush up-side the head at about sixty-five miles an hour.

They carted me off to the doctor just to be on the safe side, and the last thing I remember was Monroe swearing on his soul that it was a curve ball that just didn't break like it was supposed to. Except that when nobody was looking he wrinkled his nose at me.

That's how I felt when I saw the name of Clarence Nash listed as a part-time employee of City Delivery. Lee Sharpley had known it but hadn't said a word about it. And seeing him at the warehouse became even more unsettling.

Now for all I know it could be perfectly innocent. Perhaps he was just going beyond the call of duty to check on the progress of parolees to make sure they held to the straight and narrow. Maybe what he'd given Slick were directions to a

Benny Hinn revival. Or, at worst, maybe he wanted Slick and Dumb Eddie to fix up some of his fraternity brothers from Ohio with some fun girls for the weekend, which is an ugly inference, but what can I tell you.

"But Lance, I thought we were going to take Lance, Jr. and Tiffany to Dayton this weekend to visit my sister?"

"Sorry, dear, but my old friend Lee Sharpley hasn't been well and I need to go to Atlanta."

Then I see something that clicks in my head. It's a guy by the name of Ben Jay Delray, which to me sounds like Pig Latin, no offense. He was a foreman in City's warehouse and moved on. I do some cross-checking to find that he's working in another warehouse for about a dollar an hour less, which is considerable since Mr. Delray is married with four dependents.

So maybe he might have left for reasons other than he didn't like their coffee. And if there is anything hinky going on out there, maybe he would know about it.

I'm just getting ready to head out when my boss comes in, the back of his shirt already wringing, and calls me into his office. I go in and sit down and he takes his time about putting his stuff away, which is his way of letting me know that he's the boss. The office smells like Switzerland but he doesn't seem to notice. He unlocks his lap drawer and pulls out a file.

"A Detective Harris sent this over yesterday," he says, holding it out and letting me take hold and then not letting go of his end, as if to show me that he wants to know what's going on first. I don't mind except that his end is already getting slick and slides through his fingers like bacon through a beagle, and I know if I'm not careful he'll just make me sit there until all the humidity makes me blind.

"One of the guys who helped me keep an eye out got himself killed," I said, cradling the file in my lap and trying to dry his end on my pants without him noticing.

"We can't take personal interest in every snitch who goes belly-up," he says, which is an unfortunate choice of words on two counts and gets me a little steamed, just like the windows.

"No, sir, but if this had anything to do with things he might have been doing for me then I want to make sure it's pursued."

"The police have always done their jobs."

"With all due respect sir, the police don't give a bug's butt (there, I said it) about us and even less about guys like Ducky Nash."

I say this to let him know that I know that all the politicking and socializing he does for the sake of public relations is wasted on these people, and would be even if he didn't either bump into somebody's wife because she didn't give him a wide enough berth, or let a cocktail glass slip through his fingers and spoil somebody's rug, because he is on the side of Satan, the I.R.S.

He backs off a mite, which I appreciate.

"My only concern is for your cover. You can't jeopardize over six years of hard work because of one man no matter who he was. Besides, you don't have any legal jurisdiction in this area."

"I know that, sir, and all I wanted the write-up for was to see if there was anything that might tie him to me."

He seems to like this even though I'm lying like a new mama sow.

"Read the file," he says. "But stay out of it."

"Yes, sir," I answer. Then I leave.

I go back to my cubicle thinking that the worst thing that could happen to me wouldn't be a reprimand or even to wake up one morning to find that I had become extremely rotund and was bent toward perspiring a lot, but to discover that I had become a bureaucrat.

There's nothing in the file I didn't already know except that the butcher who killed him had done the kind of damage no civilized man would even do to an animal until it was already dead.

I also make a call to Corrections and find that yes, indeedy, Mr. Lee Sharpley is not only Dumb Eddie's parole officer, but also the parole officer for the aforementioned formerly incarcerated employee of City Delivery.

I decided to visit Mr. Delray but didn't know whether to go as a Fed or as a condom salesman. On one hand, I could send him into a panic, and on the other, he could be a deacon for the Baptists or something, and didn't want to upset him. So I decide to go as just plain Jimmy.

He lives in a little subdivision that had been new and private fifteen years ago, but now had civilization encroaching so fast with bigger houses and bigger buildings that all the residents were thinking that they might just get bulldozed over. We've got the 1996 Olympics and now everybody is wondering what's going to happen next.

There is a preacher here in town who has his own radio show and says that the Good Lord is going to return in the year 2000, and just might pick Atlanta, but I don't think we've got a chance unless Monroe gets his new indoor golf course built by then.

I pull up to the house and know right away that Mr. Delray's home because his pickup is parked in the driveway and his work shoes are parked right outside the front door. I also know that his wife keeps a clean house and he takes the line of least resistance. I knock and he comes to the door.

"Mr. Delray? I'm Jimmy Nance and I'd like to talk to you for a minute if I could."

I'm sincere and he knows I'm not selling anything when we shake because I left my satchel in the van and my hand is dry. So he steps out to oblige me.

"What can I do for you?"

"Well, sir, I know that you used to work for City Delivery and I'm looking into something that might have something to do with them," I say matter-of-factly.

"You a cop?" he asks, and I know my instincts were correct.

"Unofficial," I say, hoping to put him at ease.

He's staring at me as if he wants to get something off his chest but wondering if I'm going to do something sneaky after he tells me, like tell him I used to date his wife back in high school and then grin in a way that hurts his feelings.

Finally he points to a couple of lawn chairs near the little stoop he's got.

"I loved that job," he says, and I know he means it. "Another eighteen months and I'd have been vested in my pension," which I know to mean that what happened was the sorrow of his life.

"You know a guy named Ducky Nash?" I ask.

"Skinny, walks like a pigeon on hot asphalt?"

I nod. "He got killed last week."

"Good Lord."

"Let's hope so."

"Well, I guess you know everything ain't hunky-dory out there or you wouldn't be here," he said.

"Yes, sir."

He gets nervous and starts looking around as if whoever has gotten to him has got a spy in every tree. Then he pulls a rumpled pack of smokes from his shirt pocket, takes one out and lights it.

"If you're unofficial that mean you can't do anything?"

"No, sir. What it means is that the local cops aren't working this angle. I don't have anything to go on yet."

"And you swear you won't breathe a word it was me."

"I give you my solemn vow. What I'm hoping to do is find out something on my own and let that speak for itself."

He swallows and huffs his cigarette and I'm wondering what could have scared the poor man so bad.

"We weren't union and I had to work some holidays if enough of the businesses in town were open. So they had what you'd call a substitute day. I had a day coming from last Memorial Day and took it to do a little night fishing with my brother-in-law. He picked me up from work and I left my truck there so that I could pick it up on the way home. Well, it turned off cold so about two-thirty we decided to head in. And when we get to the warehouse I see one of the guys I know from work standing there. And he gives me some Christmas Carol about how they're doing some kind of security inspection and I can't get in. Now he don't know it but I see that he's got a gun stuck in his pants. So right away I know something's dead wrong and just turn around and go home."

"How'd you know he wasn't just messing around?"

He dropped his voice to a near-whisper. "Because he's one of the ex-cons and they aren't supposed to have guns. I got nothing personal about that, but that's when the trouble started."

"Wait a second. What do you mean, that's when the trouble started?"

"Because the place is crawling with 'em. Like I said, I got no problem with a man who's done time. But some of those guys are your capital C criminals."

"How'd all this come about."

He shook his head. "About three-four years ago this guy who I remember got sent up for robbing a couple of liquor stores gets hired. And they make him a foreman, if you can believe that. Hell, it took me eight years to make foreman. Anyway, somebody from his crew would quit or get the heave-ho and they'd hire an ex-con to take his place. It didn't take long. And all of a sudden you've got over a dozen of 'em out there and they're thick as thieves, if you'll pardon that."

"So what happened after that?"

He pauses and I can tell something has shamed him.

"I get a ride to work the next day and try to act like nothing ever happened. Except that I see some of the guys in this other crew watching me, and it gets to where I can't even take a dump in peace. Then I start finding things in my locker, which nobody is even supposed to be able to get into except me and the manager."

"What kinds of things?"

"The first thing was a picture of me with its eyes cut out. And I know something's funny because it's the same picture they took for my personnel file because I used to wear a little mustache until my wife said it chafed her. So I don't know who I can talk to and who I can't. Then I start getting notes that tell me to move on or worse things could happen. A couple of days after that I get pictures again, only this time it's pictures of my kids playing in the yard. And they've got their eyes cut out."

"So you quit."

He nods sadly. "What could I do? The personnel lady seemed real surprised and disappointed, but like I said, I didn't know who's kosher and who ain't any more."

"And you don't know what they were doing out there in the middle of the night."

He shakes his head and it sags a little. "I got no idea."

I take out a card that only has my name on it which I use to fill the gap between the one that shows me as your honest, everyday rubber man, and the one which shows me as evil incarnate. I write my home number on the back and hand it to him.

"This is my house," I say. "More than likely somebody just wanted to run you off or you would've heard from them by now. But if anything happens you aren't sure about, just give me a call."

We shake and I start to walk off and after a second he calls after me.

"Mr. Nance?"

"Jimmy."

He trots up to protect our privacy. "I was wondering if you'd consider doing me a favor."

"Sure, Mr. Delray. Anything I can."

"Something happens out there that causes enough ruckus to clean that place up, I want my old job back."

I nod and pat him on the shoulder. It wasn't his fault. Whatever is going on has got nothing to do with him.

But I drive away thinking that the truth about Ducky's death might not be found in the neighborhood at all. It might be found in a warehouse in Tucker, Georgia.

SEVEN

It's late and I'm in bed with Charlotte, which is a wholly pleasurable experience. I'm lying on my side thinking about going to sleep as soon as I can clear my head of all the things I don't want to think about, when Charlotte scrunches up and tucks herself against me, which is another wholly pleasurable experience.

Except that I'm waiting to see if she sniffs or not. If she sniffs it means she wants to talk, only since she started working around flowers and chemicals all day long she gets clogged up at the drop of a hat and it makes our relationship a real challenge. It only takes a second, though, before she does sniff and I lay like a corpse to see what happens next.

"You don't really want to have a baby, do you, Jimmy?" she whispers.

This goes through me like off-brand spaghetti but I don't know what to say. But I do know that if I heave a sigh I'm a goner, so instead I hold my breath as a safety measure until I can get a handle on things. Charlotte's serious because she waits me out, and it's not long before I have to breathe, which in my depleted condition sounds, you guessed it, just like a sigh.

"I didn't think so," she whispers again, but with a little hurt in her voice.

Then I feel her start to pull away from me and I can't have that, so I reach out my hand to stop her.

"Is it because you see so much of the ugliness in the world and wouldn't want our baby exposed to it?" she asks.

"No. I never said I—"

"Is it because you think I might have some kind of condition or something that would be passed on?" she asks, and then sniffs, and between that and the fact that she cut me off, which she never does, I know I've got to turn over.

I do and see that she's really troubled and it breaks my heart into a jillion pieces.

"Charlotte, honey, there is not one single thing wrong with you, except that sometimes I think you are too good for this world."

"Then what is it?"

"I never said I didn't want to have a baby. Why would you even think such a thing?"

"Because you don't seem...interested like usual."

"That's because of Ducky. And I'm sorry. But we've missed a few nights before."

"You sure it isn't because my fertility started for real?"

Jésus de Maria. I'd forgotten all about it.

"No, honey. I just forgot."

"A woman on Jenny Jones said that if a man knows you're fertile and won't do nothing it's because he has a subconscious aversion to fatherhood."

"Well, she doesn't know us, now does she?"

"Still..."

Have you ever had a time in your life when you knew you had to spill, but were deathly afraid to because you knew what you had to spill might make matters worse? Or that if you got started you wouldn't stop quick enough, and by then it would be too late to undo all the damage the spilling had caused? Well, there you have it.

I sighed. On purpose. Partly out of need and partly because I wanted her undivided attention.

"The idea of having a baby with you is a sweet and wonderful thing because I know how happy it would be with you as its mama."

"But...," she nudges me.

"But..."

"And..." she nudges me again, this time hard enough for me to do a quarter-turn if I wasn't so well anchored.

"And...well, the truth is, I need you, Charlotte. And I don't know if you realize that or not. And if you realize it then maybe I'm not all that thrilled with the idea. And if you don't, then maybe you won't be all that thrilled with the idea."

"I need you, too, Jimmy."

I give her a squeeze. "A person grows up and becomes what he thinks is right, and goes along every day believing that he's happy. And then something happens, in my case, you, and all of a sudden it gets cranked up so high that it makes me wonder if I was ever really happy at all. That if I wasn't just fooling myself the rest of the time. And that's scary."

"How is that scary?"

"Because I don't know which is the truly natural part, the cranked up life or the life before. And a part of me wants to know and a part of me doesn't want to know. Because if this is an unnatural part I'm still going to fight to the death to keep it because it's wonderful. But if it's really the natural part then I want to have some peace about it and not worry that it's just going to up and say adios."

"Don't you think what we have is real?" she whispers.

"Well, see, that's just it. I want to believe it is. But I don't have any kind of frame of reference, except that I can't bear the thought of seeing the day when you don't feel the same way about me, even though that is your right as a free person."

She turns over onto her back. I wish she wouldn't do that. It's distracting.

"I know what it's like to be scared. I know what it's like to wonder if there's a special place where you'll always belong or are you just there as something other folks gotta move around."

"You'll always belong with me."

"Then I need to ask you something."

"Okay."

"I need to know why you love me.

"I'm not sure I can describe all the reasons."

"If you love me because you feel sorry for me, because you think I might've gotten tromped on some day then you might be right. But there might come a time when I would want something else if only to see if I can stand on my own two feet."

"But you've already proved—"

"Shhh," she stops me. She's picked up a new habit and I'm not sure it's such a good deal. "But if you love me because you see something in me that maybe you think nobody else sees, and it's extra special in your eyes, and is part of the reason you feel good most of the time, then it's real."

"It's just like that," I whisper.

Then she looks at me and even in the dark I can see how serious she is, and there is a wisdom in her face that I've never seen before, and not because I ever, ever thought she was slow, but because she is so quiet and light-hearted most of the time. And I gotta tell you that it scares the Hell out of me.

"Anybody can love just about anybody else at one time or another because everybody's got things in common," she says. "But if a person loves what's important to another person, and believes in that person, then you've got something to build on."

I felt ashamed. I wasn't sure I even knew what was important to her in that sense.

"What's important to you, Charlotte?"

"Us," she said.

"I believe in that," I said.

"Then why ain't I pregnant yet, you slacker?" she giggled.

"I got no clue."

I reached over and pulled her close and nuzzled my face against her neck.

"And you don't think a baby will change any of that?" I asked.

"On the outside, maybe, but not on the inside. Remember when you took me roller skating because I wanted to even though you couldn't roller skate a lick?"

"My butt was blue for a week."

"Remember what you told me?"

"Ow?"

"You said it was the company that made all the difference, not the activity."

She's got me there. "Charlotte, honey, you are the joy and sorrow of my life."

"I know that," she says, and gives me a big kiss.

We fall asleep like that and I feel more safe and warm than I have in a long time, maybe ever, and have dreams about little boys who grow up with hands big enough to palm a basketball and little girls who grow up to run the F.B.I.

Which is why I'm completely discombobulated when the alarm goes off at three o'clock in the morning. I jump out of bed like I'm late for breakfast and whip on my underwear and grab for my pants. Then I hear Charlotte snicker.

"Jimmy, honey, you've got a hole in your butt."

"Of course I do, darlin'."

"No, you goof. You've got your drawers on backwards."

Which in fact, I did.

This was the third night in a row I'd done this. I'd been getting up in the dead of night and driving all the way out to Tucker only to find City's warehouse looking like a graveyard the night after a funeral.

But tonight when I drive by I see someone standing at the gate, and just keep on going without so much as a how do-you-do. Except that I park a couple hundred yards down in a chiropractor's parking lot and backtrack on foot.

I find the fence that encircles the entire perimeter of City's property and move like a ghost until I can get a good peep at the gate. Sure enough, some guy is standing guard out there. I don't know if he's got a gun but I ain't about to ask him.

I crouch and wait for a spell, opening and closing my hands, stretching my fingers, and thinking that if I had hands like Patrick Ewing I could've started for Bobby Knight at Indiana.

By half-time of the National Championship game I've got twenty-six points and Bobby gives me a big hug. Mid-way through the second half I take a cheap foul and Bobby runs out onto the court and pours a quart of Gatorade down the referee's pants. He gets slapped with a technical but the fans go hooty-wild. We're behind by one with four seconds to go and I've got the ball at the free throw line with two shots. I make the first. Bobby blows me a kiss and the crowd starts chanting 'Jim-my! Jim-my!' I get ready for the winning shot. I bow my head for a second. I look up...

...and see a big eighteen-wheeler pull up to the gate with the Wal-Mart logo painted on its side. It gets waved through in a hurry and then the guard resumes his vigilance. I've got to move. Sorry, Bobby.

I sprint toward the corner of the fence. I'm going great and thinking that maybe I could've played in the NBA small hands and all. They've got a guy who plays for the Hornets named Muggsy Bogues who I don't think could whip Mrs. Bocook in a fair fight.

Then I take a tree limb across the forehead and that way-lays me. I'm far enough from the gate to know that the guy didn't hear me and there doesn't seem to be anyone else keeping watch. So I round the corner and high-tail it down the fenceline which should bring me to a point about a hundred yards from the terminal, but still back in the woods.

I get there and can't see a damned thing through the maze of parked trucks and vans except part of the front-end of the Wal-Mart truck backed up to a dock.

I hate it for all I'm worth but I've got to climb the fence. I do this hoping they don't have Dobermans running loose and all those special parts promised to my Chosen won't end up as kibble. She'd never believe I could do something so stupid.

I surprise myself with how good of shape I'm in, relatively speaking, even if I did get knocked on my caboose and still took the charge. So I'm over without major incident. No 'Hey, there's a guy over there with a knot on his forehead!' or anything like that. And I move to a position behind a van that lets me watch the dock from safety.

And I am utterly amazed.

I don't know if you remember life before ESPN. Before

Australian Rules Football, Hurling, Curling and Tandem Underwater Pinch-and-Go. But back in those ancient times we had to rely on Jim McKay and ABC's Wide World of Sports for such delicacies.

I watched it faithfully, except that I would always excuse myself to comb my hair or something during the opening because I thought it was a shame how they embarrassed that poor ski-jumper every week. How could the poor man even walk down the street after that.

"Hey, I know you. You're 'Agony of Defeat' Thorsen, ain't ya?"

Monroe's favorite was the Armwrestling Championships from Petaluma, California, since you could always count on a broken arm or two.

Mine were the speed sports.

I used to think that the fastest people in all of sport were the guys who worked the pits at car races. They moved so fast they looked like Tokyo with Godzilla on the loose.

Then I saw the Fireman's Drag Races.

In the Fireman's Drag Races you had teams of firemen from all over the country hanging onto souped-up fire trucks for dear life, screaming down a drag strip until they reached the general vicinity of a hydrant. Then they would all jump off, sliding and tumbling every which way since most of the time the fire truck was still moving, and flopping like fish at low tide until they could get organized enough to get the hose hooked up and spewing. The fastest spewers were the winners, of course, even though I always wondered if the folks back home felt any more secure after watching them.

But this is exactly what it looked like on the dock. Teams of two unloaded the truck—reminding me of the time Monroe got invited to dinner on the grounds at the Ebeneezer Baptist Church, who called a meeting afterward and decided that they really didn't much care if he got the Spirit or not when it came right down to it—and plopped cartons onto pallets, where forklifts moving like bumper cars hustled them back into the warehouse. It took less than ten minutes to empty the trailer.

I couldn't see far into the warehouse, but I did notice that the cartons contained T.V's, VCR's, stereos and microwaves. And all the movers I recognized were ex-cons, including Dumb Eddie, who seemed to be one of the foremen of this operation, believe it or not, and Slick, who stood by and leaned up against a post and didn't budge until the warehouse was locked up tighter than Mrs. Bocook's pocketbook.

Then Eddie gets into the driver's side of the cab, Slick rides shotgun and everybody else scatters.

I know I have to follow them and they've got the jump on me. I make the fence fine and hurtle myself toward the chiropractor's office thinking that being born with Shirley Temple's hands wouldn't have been so bad if I'd had Bob Hayes' legs. I'm also thinking that when this is all over I might come back and give that chiropractor some business.

I'm gasping and heaving like I've got the numbies, but they've got me by at least forty-five seconds, so I jump in and floor it in the direction of the Interstate, knowing that if they'd come the other way I'd have seen them. I'm doing fifty by the time I hit City's property, sixty when I pass the gate, seventy when I'm clear, and look in the rearview mirror...

...and see the tractor-trailer pull out with Slick's purple-esque Gremlin right behind it. So how was I supposed to know they had to stop?

I stay in front because I don't want to arouse suspicion and have about a half-mile lead when we approach the Interstate. I'm thinking that they're probably going to head south toward town and take that exit. Except that I see them taking the exit north and I know I'm in trouble.

I'm going to have to backtrack in a hurry and that's a Hell of a lot easier said than done since Atlanta is the cloverleaf capital of the world. Architects and designers the world over come just to stare in awe and amazement at all the elegant and perfectly symmetrical ways we've created to get people lost.

One bit of folklore tells of some old boy from Ontario who

was headed for Florida back in 1984, and who took this very exit looking for a place to whizz and was never heard from again. They say that especially on rainy nights you can hear an airy, distant voice crying, "Where's the bathroom, *eh*?"

By the time I'm heading north again I've not only lost sight of Dumb Eddie and Slick, but am dizzy from the cloverleaf. Just like the time I rode the Tilt-A-Whirl with Tammy Parsons back in ninth grade. Petey was nowhere to be seen so I sneaked off behind the Fun House to get sick. Trouble was that Tammy's big sister Mavis was back there with Toby Wheless, and if he hadn't slipped in what I'd just deposited I'd have probably ended up looking more like the youngest boy on My Three Sons.

I'm doing eighty and my van is starting to shimmy, just like Mavis as I recall. I'm just about to give up hope when I see the turnoff to I-75 North. And there in the distance climbing the offramp is a tractor-trailer followed by something with taillights that look like a critter out of a Roger Corman movie, and I know I've hit paydirt.

I followed them for about an hour and was beginning to think they were headed for Canada. Maybe the old boy who was looking for a place to whizz had possessed them. Then they take the Dalton exit, the Carpet Capital of the World, and just as a matter of geographical accuracy is only spitting distance from the Tennessee state line. They drive all the way through Dalton, and frankly, I'm grateful it's dark, until they turn off onto a back road. I wait until they're out of sight before I follow. And there about two miles in they just abandon the truck.

I know this because the Gremlin lists severely to one side when Dumb Eddie gets in, and rocks itself back into place.

I turned around and beat it outta there, wanting to get a good lead for the trip home.

So I knew something. Somebody, presumably Dumb Eddie and Slick, had hi-jacked a Wal-Mart truck and stored its contents in the warehouse of City Delivery. Then the two aforementioned miscreants had driven the ill-fated truck out into the boonies and abandoned it.

All in all it had been a productive night. So I stopped in a twenty-four hour BP station near Calhoun and treated myself to a Honey Bun and some chocolate milk for the ride home.

EIGHT

The next day I'm so tired I can't chew straight and wondering what I should do next. I've also realized that the operation out at City's warehouse had been carefully planned as to a specific time. I'm also thinking that between chasing your criminal element in the middle of the night and trying to honor the dreams of my Beloved, which I admit I don't need much encouragement, I need some rest or I'm going to die.

So I decide to play a hunch and call City's office on the sly again. I get the same lady as before but know that she won't recognize my voice since she probably talks to fifty guys a day who sound just like me.

"I was out walking my dog the other night and he got away from me and shinnied under your fence—"

"Must've been a Hell of a walk," she says. "There ain't a house within two miles of here."

"I was going to meet a buddy of mine who's a chiropractor and has his office out your way." Quick, ain't I?

Then she starts to coo on me.

"That man's a saint. One of them quacks in town said I had an irregular coccyx and I come to find out it was just a backache. That man saved my marriage."

"So I try to get him out but can't get in," I say, trying to get it all out before I lose my place.

"You mean we still got your dog in here somewhere?"

"No, ma'am. I just want to make sure it doesn't happen again."

"Then keep him away from here on Monday's because that's the security man's night off. The rest of the time there's somebody around." Then she pauses and I can hear her thinking to herself that she really don't know me and maybe has been too loose with the beans. "Of course we've got alarms and other stuff for when he ain't here."

"That's very wise," I answer. "And I hope I haven't been an inconvenience."

"You thought about castration?"

It was almost as if she read my mind. "Ma'am?"

"The dog. Have him neutered and he won't run off like that."

"Oh. Well, it's so that I've gotten used to him the way he is and don't want to hurt his feelings."

"I know just what you mean," she says. "I feel the same way about my old man."

There's an old saying in our business that goes 'when in doubt, follow the money'. It's good advice but a lot easier said than done, even for me, and especially when you don't know who's got the money to start with.

But I do know that even if Dumb Eddie and Slick don't have the money, you can bet your Aunt Mary's rose bushes they have at least a peripheral association with it. And so I think that maybe I should do some more checking on Dumb Eddie.

Finding somebody when you're a Fed is so easy it ought to be a crime, which it would be if you did it the way I did.

Dumb Eddie lives just off Polk Street in an ancient neighborhood near downtown. It's the kind of neighborhood that when the houses were first built everybody was proud just to be a part of it all, but which now made some people wish they'd paid more attention in school so maybe they wouldn't be stuck there. It's neat and clean and not run down as much as it is scaled small.

Dumb Eddie's house was an old white frame job with a screened-in porch the size of a doormat and maybe six rooms if you count the john. It wasn't exactly Beverly Hills and Eddie's grass needed mowing. Still, I was a little surprised in that it was a family neighborhood and Dumb Eddie looked more the single-wide trailer type. But what the hey, how did I know he wasn't a great Santy for the kiddies come Christmas time.

There was an alleyway two houses down and that's where I parked. This was an alley from the old days. An alley that had never tasted asphalt and was really just a couple of ruts that operated as a buffer zone between the butt-ends of people's yards, most of which had some kind of untamed growth to provide privacy.

This was an alley that no criminal had lurked around in, except maybe for some kids with spray paint who adorned the sides of garages with things like 'Class of 75 Rules' or 'Sally Scott did the deed with Georgie Pope on this spot', or the guy I happen to see piddling with his lawnmower in his skivvies across the way.

I'm sitting there thinking and trying to talk myself out of doing what I'm thinking about. What I'm thinking about is snooping around Dumb Eddie's place in such a way as to leave nothing to the imagination, which would make me and Dumb Eddie colleagues no matter how much righteous talk goes on in my head since I don't have a warrant.

But I need to know and all the talking to myself in the world isn't going to change that. So I see an empty garage opened up to the alley a few houses down and poke the back end of my van in there until it's hidden from view. I stick a note on my windshield that says 'ran out of gas' just in case somebody comes home, even though I know they might wonder how, if I ran out of gas, I coasted backward halfway up an alley and into their garage.

In my lockbox with my gun I have a few pairs of those thin latex gloves doctors use but am embarrassed to have to tell you why.

Sometimes in my profession, and I mean my other profession, I am called upon to dispose of...trade-ins. I don't really know how this happens, and to be honest it bothers me to even think about it, wondering if maybe some soul availed himself of my wares and then used it right there on the premises, but hardly a day goes by when I don't find at least one second-hand condom in the vicinity of one of my machines.

Maybe it's a case like Grady Tutwiler, who has some legitimate reason to be dissatisfied with the product, except that these are never laundered. Or it could be a protest from some Holy Roller who believes that if the Good Lord had wanted to stop the river from flowing, so to speak, He'd have had something built-in. Or maybe it's like those poor misspent creatures whose heads hang in Monroe's den and even with the glass eyes carry with them a look of utter astonishment, that it's some kind of trophy. Whatever the reason, I am forced to carry these gloves.

This also makes it easier to do what I've got to do and know that I won't leave any fingerprints.

Since I'm wearing my work clothes, which are green work pants and a white shirt with a patch that says 'Jimmy' over my pocket, and look every bit like I could be the cable man or there to fix the washer, I decide to take the direct approach and walk right across the yard straight to Eddie's back door as if I've got every right in the world to be there.

There aren't any cars or other signs of life, and the back door is almost completely sheltered from view, so I knock. Twice. Just to be on the safe side. When no one answers I know I'm safe unless some Jehovah's Witness shows up and takes issue with me for working his territory and pokes me one.

The only other thing is that I hear this strange gurgling sound, like a commode's running except that it would have to be one Hell of a commode to be so loud. Then I think about how hard it was for Dumb Eddie to squeeze into the Gremlin and pause to snicker to myself before returning to commit my first felony with malice aforethought.

I did commit a misdemeanor once even though it was all Monroe's fault. We were in Woolworth's with Mama and Monroe comes over and says,

"Let's see who can cob the biggest thing without getting caught."

I swear I didn't want any part of it but I see Monroe standing over by the candles and there's a whole batch of 'em that look like the Washington Monument. So he picks one up and slides it down his pants, and then makes a face at me.

I know he's thinking that nobody would dare look down his pants and that anybody who would even peek would come away with the idea that the Fates had just been kind to him, especially since he'd just hit puberty and all. So he just stands there by the door grinning while Mama goes through the check-out line.

And then I stroll up with a punchball. It was one of those heavy-duty balloon things with a long, heavy-duty rubber band tied to it. But it was bigger than Monroe's head and far bigger than his measly little candle. I stand right there beside him, figuring that anybody who saw me, and me so innocent looking besides, would just think that nobody would be so stupid as to try to steal something so big right out in the open.

Nobody says a word to us and Monroe is boiling as we walk to the car. Mama doesn't even seem to notice and I know I made out like a bandit, which of course, I did.

Monroe was always a sorry loser and he takes the punchball away from me and starts frammin' it right there in the car with Mama driving, anticipating the results.

"Monroe, stop frammin' that infernal ball," she says.

"It ain't mine," he says, shoving it to me. "It's Jimmy's."

Mama drives on for a minute and then gives me the hawk eye in the rear view mirror.

"Jimmy, where'd you get that punchball?"

I know I've had it. "At Woolworth's. Didn't you see me?" And if you'd heard me you'd have thought I'd just come from choir practice.

"I didn't see you pay for it," she says.

"Well, I kinda didn't this time around," I answer. "I left my money at home. I'll make good on it next time."

She skids the car to a halt and backhands me one. Then she drives back to Woolworth's and makes me go up to the manager and give him the ball and confess that I stole it. He looks at me real stern and gives me a lecture on honesty, which would have been bad enough except that we interrupted his lunch of liver and onions and he blew fumes worse than our barn at me the whole time.

Then she jerks me all the way back to the car and tells me that she's going to make sure Daddy gives me a wallop when we get home. Monroe's all stitched up from trying to keep from laughing out loud and making gooney faces at me, and I think I'm going to cry.

Except that Mama is so upset she doesn't slow down for the railroad tracks and there's about eight sets which she takes at forty miles-an-hour. We bump so hard that the candle up and pokes Monroe in the parts of himself which have just gone through the change and he pukes all over the back seat. And Mama forgets all about the punchball and concentrates on making Monroe spend the afternoon cleaning the car. Even so, nobody would ride in it for a week.

I manage to snatch the candle when he's in the bathroom cleaning himself off, and hold it for leverage. We called it even.

Eddie's door has a single bolt and I know that all I have to do is slip my penknife in there and make a little space between the latch and the hole, which I do, and the door slides open. Except that there's a chain on the door and the gurgling gets louder.

The chain has a lot of slack in it and I'm wondering if maybe I can just slide it off from the outside with the door ajar like it is. So I stick my left hand through and find the little knob and hold the door with my right hand to keep it as still as possible.

I slide the chain as far as I can, but unfortunately it's not enough. The door is as tight as I can get it without doing permanent damage to my arm. I shift and wraggle it around and push the door even tighter, and manage to move the chain a fraction more, but it's not enough.

I'm thinking that this might be an operation like removing a bandage, even though I hate the idea.

I cut my leg on a barbed-wire fence once and by the time it had healed all the hair had grown back. So the nurse, who looked like Fred Gwynne and had probably been told that once since she scowled all the time, said that the best way was to just yank it off in one fell swoop and be done with it. She did and the last thing I saw before losing consciousness was Herman Munster giving me an evil smile.

I'm debating that if I push the door hard just long enough to slide the chain the extra half-inch I need, can I take the pain? I decide, shoot yeah. I brace myself and hold my breath and push.

I might have been able to take the pain but I couldn't take the pinch. Somehow a chunk of the skin that hangs loose between your armpit and your elbow, and does this no matter how much you work out, got caught in the door and that was all she wrote. I yelled louder than the Clap of Creation and jerked the door off my arm.

I immediately looked around to see if I'd been discovered, thinking that I might as well have put one of those flashing signs out by the road like they use at Ford dealerships that say *Remember Pearl Harbor*, only that in my case it would say *Burglar at Work. Call Police*. But I was shielded by the sound of the guy mowing grass in his baby blue Hanes.

And then when I look back the door is standing wide open with the chain dangling there all innocent as if to give me the 'says you'.

I go inside and close the door and fix the chain back, which to my relief is virtually undamaged, but which to my shame I discover that what I had tried to do is physically impossible since the extra slack was just an illusion. But then the gurgling sound burps at me and I jump and whirl in a panic.

And just about fall out.

It's a hot tub. An honest-to-God hot tub, and a whopper,

too. In fact there wasn't any room for anything else. That back room was just a little built-on from the time many moons ago when the modern versions of washers and dryers came along and somebody convinced us all that we should have separate facilities for such purposes.

But that's what it was. A hot tub in full bloom. And knowing Dumb Eddie, and having that kind of image in my head, which frankly would be unkind to describe, and seeing the large wet ring all around it where he had proved the theory of displacement many, many times, just about made me giggle except that I knew this was just the beginning.

I tiptoed through the house, the inside being like the outside and as common as dirt. It didn't take long to find what I was looking for.

The kitchen was thick with gadgets. There were two microwaves, about four different kinds of food processors, and even an espresso maker, which seemed just as ridiculous as the hot tub until I caught a whiff and saw that Eddie was using it for brewing ice tea.

There was a double refrigerator-freezer that did every thing but wipe your nose and both were stuffed to capacity. There was even a mini-keg and beer dispenser.

The living room was worse. There was one of those giant six-foot T.V.'s along one wall, a stereo system that made me think Eddie had once been a roadie for the Grateful Dead and had done a little shoplifting for spite when they gave him his walking papers. And there was a pinball machine.

This wasn't one of those cheap knockoffs, either. This was a full-size, drinkin' man's bar kind of pinball machine, with a big cartoon image of Madonna on it, which reminded me of the pictures on my men's room machines, though I doubted any of those girls made anywhere near fifty million dollars a year.

There was another big color television devoted strictly to video games and one of those baseketball games you see in sports bars where you can make a bunch of free throws with a midget basketball and win free games. I knew it well. The ball was small enough for me to palm.

There was a ton more, but all-in-all the place looked like a manic depressive had cut loose with a Penney's catalogue on a two-week high.

I knew what I had come to find out. I was looking at maybe eighty thousand dollars' worth of stuff. Dumb Eddie had money he didn't want anybody to know about, and like all good Americans, was laundering it in a way that was almost untraceable, by making large cash purchases. Stocking a funhouse might not be your idea of adventurous living, but it suited Dumb Eddie.

So I knew something else. The hijacked goods were being turned over and Eddie was in it for big profit. I still didn't know how or where Ducky fit into all this, but deep down I knew and it bothered me. I didn't picture Dumb Eddie as a killer, but money does weird things to people. Just ask anybody in Congress.

I'm wrung out and feeling pretty puny and decide to go home and take a nap before Charlotte gets home. Except that when I get there Mrs. Bocook is out in her yard and waves me over. I can't help it but my chin bobs a little. She's a good sixty yards away but sees it.

"Ah, don't be such a pansy, Jimmy," she calls out. "I know you're here to catch up on your sleep. This won't take long."

I walk over and see that she's got one of those weed whackers and is doing some serious damage around her sidewalk. She's got this odd little grin on her face and to be honest, it's frightening to watch. Give her a hockey mask and she could be a star.

She stops when I get there but points the thing in my direction, which makes me do a little hop back the way I came.

"Aren't you skittish," she says.

"Well, I haven't been sleeping too good lately, Mrs. Bocook," I say politely.

"That's what I want to talk to you about. I know what you're up to and you're going about it all wrong."

I hate to think it but I'm wondering if maybe Charlotte hasn't told her too much about my business.

"Ma'am?"

"You're trying to put Charlotte in the family way, are you not?"

"Oh, that."

"Well, you're going about it all wrong. To get it done right the first go 'round you got to work your angles."

I can't believe what I'm hearing.

"Ah, Mrs. Bocook."

"Dammit, Jimmy, don't be such a Christian. We all know how it works. And unless you're endowed like a stud horse the regular way is just going to frustrate things because you won't have the distance and all your little soldiers will up and die long before they make it to the fort. Now the best way for you may be to turn her over doggie-style and get her at a good downward angle—"

"Good Lord, Mrs. Bocook," I say. I hated to interrupt her but what choice did I have. "Ain't this a little personal?"

She gives me a look like she's fixing to crank up the weed whacker and take all the guesswork out of my manhood once and for all.

"Now, Jimmy. It's a perfectly natural process. When poor old Mr. Bocook, God love him, had the will but not the way, I used to massage his saddle bags with a little Deep Heat. Now's not the time to think about how Holy the 'how' is. Screw it. You've got that little girl to think about and she's determined. I can see it in her eyes."

I give up. "Yes, ma'am. I'll give it careful thought."

Then she smiles at me, which she never does. "Enjoy it while you can, boy," she says. And that's that.

I go up to the loft and get naked between the sheets, which I've got to tell you is a wonderful feeling even if Charlotte isn't there. It's not long before I'm off.

Except that I have this dream. And in it Mrs. Bocook is standing at the foot of the bed screeching out instructions to Charlotte and me. It's so unnerving that I wake up...

...and see Mrs. Bocook standing at the foot of the bed grinning down at me.

"Aaaaagh!" And I sit up with a start.

Charlotte jumps a foot up and a foot back, all at the same time. I see that it's her but my heart's beating so fast that I have to take a minute to calm down. She inches a little closer.

"Sorry," she says, and I can tell her feelings are hurt a little. "I was just checking on you. I tried to be quiet."

I nod. "I know. I thought you were Mrs. Bocook."

"Now what would Mrs. Bocook be doing up here with you all naked and asleep in the bed."

"She wouldn't, honey. I just had a bad dream is all. I'm sorry if I spooked you."

Then she comes over and sits down beside me. She reaches over and gives me a little peck on the cheek, mindful of how sensitive I am about my mouth when I first wake up, and I reach over and put my hand on her leg, which is a fair trade if I ever heard one.

"It's six o'clock. Want some supper?"

I'd slept five hours and it felt like five minutes. "In a little bit. Let me wake up first."

She gets a little flushed in the cheeks and smiles in the ways she does that lets me know she's up to something. Then she pulls the sheet up and peeks in.

"Seems to me that you're already awake."

And I know that you know what happens next, so there's no point in beating a dead horse, so to speak. Except that later when I'm lying there holding her and maybe even beginning to doze off again she tilts her head to look at me.

"Jimmy?"

"Hmmm?"

"That dream you were having when I came in..."

"Yeah?"

"What did you mean when you said 'Flip her over, Son, you ain't no stud horse!'?"

NINE

I do some more nosing around in the computer on City Delivery, cross-referencing corporate tax returns with personal tax returns until I came up with the name of Eric Tannenbaum, who I know to be the real honcho. Mr. Tannenbaum is not somebody I know, but as far as I can tell he never did so much as stick his tongue out at his mama.

He's as clean as Rudy's toilets, and that's saying something since Rudy is extra prideful about his premises and won't let any of the local riffraff even take a pee in there.

"You can't judge a man by the color of his skin, his religion, what he does for a living or what kind of car he drives," he told me once. "But you can always tell the bent of a man's character by how he keeps his bathroom."

Some day when I am free to tell Rudy all the things I want to tell him, I'm going to mention the bidet I found in Dumb Eddie's bathroom. Then I'm going to tell him he's using it as a water fountain.

My route is uneventful except that at Toby's Exxon, which is a real treat because it's one of the few remaining full-service gas stations around where you can sit out and chew the fat and drink a bottle of pop and watch cars go by, and it won't cost you anything but the price of the pop, I have a little shock.

Somebody has taped a picture of Jesus above one of my machines. It's that picture of Him on the cross, looking so forlorn and dejected, as if to let us know that He knew all along we'd end up this way. Below it was a card that had *Fornicators Beware!* written on it.

Now how does anyone really know that my condoms are being used for such purposes.

I've got one customer who uses them to keep his minnows in when he does a little river fishing. The water in the bait bucket would get too warm and when the minnows would hit the river they'd die of shock before even the first nibble. So he filled a few fleshtone Regulars with water, put the minnows in, and dangled them in the river to become acclimated before giving their all in the cause of sport.

I've got another customer who took one of my Ribbed and blew it up with helium and made a model of a blowfish for his boy's science project, and it took third prize. It might've taken first if the teacher hadn't asked him why it had a nose and the boy could've told her.

I was twenty-eight years old when I met Charlotte. Before her I can count the women I'd gotten serious with on one hand. I think some people have got it all wrong. We aren't savages and we aren't always on the prowl. We're trying to find something real and tangible and sometimes we have to touch in order to do that.

I read once where somebody said that sex is a beginning for a woman and an ending for a man. What horse hockey. If sex was the ending then we sure as Hell wouldn't come back for more, now would we. I think that's part of the corner we've backed ourselves into. Thinking in terms of men and women instead of people, and it's hurting us all.

People want three things in life. They want affection. They want companionship. And they want to be understood.

At least I get to eat at Rudy's today. I walk in and do my business, grateful that there are two bathrooms I can still go into without having to worry. Unless you count the time I accidentally walked in on Reverend Patterson's wife, Eula, who didn't hear me on account of she was right in the middle of the sixth verse of *Just As I Am*, and the echo in her stall was considerable. Naturally I tried to remove myself from the premises without being detected so that she wouldn't think she'd been violated and start in screaming, except that Eula's friend, Tessie, walks in right behind me and looks at me and hears the singing and stoops down to see Eula's feet under the stall tapping in time with the music.

I think I'm in serious jeopardy until Tessie pats me one and walks over and pounds on the stall, which sounds just like a jet bottomed out.

"Get it done quick, Eula," she says. "You're keeping Jimmy from his lunch."

I'm petrified and ain't about to say anything.

"You out there, Jimmy?" Eula asks, as if nothing is, has ever been, or will ever be wrong with the world.

"Ma'am?" which in solemn truth is all I can muster.

"Go on and do your business. I'll be out in a jiffy."

And if it's true that some good comes out of every situation, I know that if they ever put changing out condom machines in the Olympics, I'm as good as gold.

"Red bean, Jimmy?" Rudy asks when I sit in my customary place.

"Think I'll have the chicken salad today."

Then Rudy stops in his tracks and comes to stare at me.

"Good Lord. You look like yesterday's twilight paper."

"I'm a little tired, I guess," I say.

"And that ain't all," he says in agreement. "You know I make the worst chicken salad in Georgia. Let me give you a big old liver sandwich to get your blood going."

I shake my head and it's all I can do to hold down a burp. I've never been able to eat any organ from any animal ever since the time in Biology class when we had to watch a movie that showed some geek in a crewcut dissect a fetal pig, during which Petey passes me a note that says,

'Wanna JuJube?'

"How about a plain old chicken sandwich then?"

"Okay."

"And some hot mustard potato salad. That's one of my specialties."

I nod but my heart ain't in it.

Rudy serves my lunch and pulls up to keep me company. I

have to love him for it because he's thinking I'm low and is only doing what any friend would do, even though I know we all fall short from time to time. But I can't talk to him about what's really bothering me.

"Heard about Ducky Nash," he says.

"Yeah, I figured you had."

"And I know that he would like it knowing that there's somebody taking it hard."

"I found him, Rudy."

Rudy nods at me then as if he understands perfectly and nothing more need be said. Then he pulls in closer like he always does when he wants to give me the straight dope.

"There's talk around that he was into something bad. And not just penny-ante stuff either."

This gets my attention even though I've already got an inclination about what it is. He goes on.

"There's talk that some bad boys have been poking around his business, too, like maybe he left something undone behind him and they want to clean it up before it gets them in trouble."

"You know who?" I ask.

Rudy shakes his head. "Stay out of it, Jimmy. Grieve if you got to, but stay out of it. Ducky don't need the company that bad." Then he smiles.

I smile, too, even though I've got a hole in my stomach from all the secrets I keep from him.

"So how's Charlotte?" he asks after a moment.

I smile for real. I can't help myself.

"She wants to have a baby."

"And she's counting on you to put her in a motherly way, I suppose."

"Yeah. She is."

Rudy gets up and starts back down the counter, shaking his head.

"Should've had the liver," he says.

I drive over to Ducky's building after lunch and start looking around. I find out that Ducky's room has already been rented and that the only stuff left other than what the police took was in a box downstairs.

The old guy who looks out for the place has the blackest skin of any human being I've ever seen. He also has little white tufts of hair just above his ears and hardly any elsewhere, and in truth reminds me of Uncle Remus, which I would never say in a million years and wouldn't even think if I hadn't loved that old Walt Disney movie so much before people said it was wrong.

He lets me look in Ducky's box and I don't even have to flash my badge, except that I see right off just how pitiful it is. There's a couple of old worn out shirts and a gold suit covered with sparkles that looks like it was left over from the disco era, and which probably had been the pride of his life once. The pockets are all empty and I move on to an old billfold, which is also empty as if I couldn't guess, except for a couple of pictures. One is in a place of honor by itself in the inside flap.

It's an old black & white showing a kid of about seven or eight, which I knew to be Ducky on account of his feet looked like a penguin's, and a heavy-set woman who couldn't have been more than thirty but smiled without showing teeth, and had eyes a million years old.

I pulled out the picture and there was a date on the back. 6-11-92. There was also a phone number and I thought it was nice that he tried to keep in touch.

I started to put the picture back and something hit me. I stared at it the same way I do at the computer, waiting for something to click. Then it happened. It was the date. This picture had to have been at least thirty years old.

Then I felt myself smiling. The date was about the time Ducky made parole. Only a handful of people would have remembered it. I was one of them.

I wrote down the number and put the billfold back. On my way out I saw Uncle Remus sitting out on the porch, his eyes closed, no doubt spinning wonderful stories in his head. I almost asked him if I could sit at his feet and listen for a spell.

Instead I said, “Excuse me?”

He looked and except for his eyes he could’ve been a statue.

“I left the box where it was. I was just wondering, anybody else come around here looking in Ducky’s stuff?”

“Police,” he said, and only his lips moved.

“Other than them.”

He studied me for a moment to see if I was worthy and I never doubted for a second he would be right.

“Boy about the size of a bus and some weasley little knob that runs the show.”

Dumb Eddie and Slick.

Have you ever been worried about something and then found out that what you were worried about wasn’t worth worrying about, but because of it you had new things to worry about that only made matters worse?

Like back when our former President Reagan found a knot in his entrails. I had been experiencing similar discomfort and was sure I had colon cancer. So I went to this Internist, and what he did to me to check this out I won’t say except to tell you that I hope you never have to worry about it, and he told me that I didn’t have colon cancer but did have a severe case of hemorrhoids. So it turned out to be a double-edged sword, pardon the metaphor.

And I had to carry this little innertube around with me to sit on, and it got so bad that I ended up having to start each conversation with,

“It’s not what you’re thinking. I was chosen at random to test a new product for Goodyear. The Grand Prize winner gets to ride in the blimp with John Madden.”

So now I’m worried that maybe Ducky was a part of the illegal goings-on out at City Delivery and wasn’t going to say anything to me about it, except that something went bad wrong and then it was too late.

I go to a phone booth and call the number. It’s still in service and it sounds like a kid who answers. I don’t know how to play this, so I decide to just play it by ear.

"Hello, my name is Jimmy Nance and—"

"Where you been?"

"Uh, beg pardon?"

"Jeez, it took you long enough. Glad you ain't watchin' out for me. Well, I guess you better come on over."

He gave me the address and it was only a few blocks over, so I was there in five minutes. I pulled up in front of an old house the same vintage as Ducky's except that this was a single-family. I could see old newspapers lining the walls inside.

Outside was this tall gawky kid with glasses and a Michael Jordan T-shirt. He was only about eleven or twelve and he grinned at me with a ball under his arm. I clapped my hands and he tossed it to me and I did a couple of tricks. I gave him a bounce pass back and he stuck it where it had come from.

"Hands too small," I say by way of explanation. "Couldn't palm the ball."

"Being white probably didn't help," he answered.

Which may very well have been true, but which was out of my jurisdiction.

"Jimmy Nance," I said, and shook his hand.

"Arnold Carvey," he said. "They call me 'Tops'. I'm only five-ten now but I'm headed for six-eight, six-nine."

We move back toward the house and sit on the concrete block they've got for a stoop. I'm trying to figure out how this kid knew to expect me since I didn't know as much myself.

"You the G-Man, right?" he asks. I didn't know what to say.

"Ducky was my uncle," he explains. "Well, he was really like a third cousin or something, but we was the only family he had hereabouts."

"Sorry for your loss," I said.

"Mine ain't near as bad as his," he says, which was entirely true. "Anyway, he comes in a couple of weeks ago all nervous and shit and says that if anything happens to him a white man who looks dumb but really ain't, and is really some kind of G-Man besides might come around looking into it. He says if he don't show just to let it go, but if he shows I got to give him something."

I perk up. Wouldn't you?

"What is it?"

He shakes his head and looks downright disgusted. So I reach into my pocket and pull out my badge.

"You know I'm undercover," I said. "I've got to trust you. Just like I trusted Ducky."

"You could trust me a lot more if you let me hold some of them rubbers Ducky said you carry around with you."

"You look a little young to be doing that kind of courtin'," I say.

He looks disgusted again. "I'm talking free enterprise," he says with a grin. "I can get a dollar a pop for 'em at school."

I go to the van and get him a carton which holds twenty-four.

"Mixed colors," I say. "Should be worth more than a buck apiece."

He takes them and puts them in his shirt and I'm wondering if I'm not contributing to something I might live to regret, but then again it's not dope.

He fishes into his pocket and comes up with a key.

"This is it?" I ask.

"That's it," he answers.

"What's it to?" I ask.

"You the G-Man," he says. "Figure it out."

And then he turns around and goes inside.

I didn't have the heart to tell him that I was just a mid-grade civil servant with bad aim. Ducky had overestimated me. It was a padlock key that could have fit any of ten billion padlocks in the universe. Even by eliminating everywhere but Atlanta, there must have been seven or eight hundred thousand locks in the Greater Metropolitan area. And all I had to do is find the one this key fit.

I noticed that there was a bicycle chained to a tree next

door and tried the key in its lock. It didn't work. One down, seven hundred ninety-nine thousand nine hundred ninety-nine to go.

Actually I'm probably underestimating myself. I could narrow it down to a couple thousand places, a couple hundred a few years ago before everybody got the urge to store stuff instead of dispose of it, which is what is done to it eventually, and all these mini-warehouses sprang up like toadstools in a cow pie.

Mini-warehouses are the utter bane of Feds anyway, since they're so hard to trace. If all the mini-warehouses in America were searched on any given day, the ultimate proceeds would knock the Federal Debt from four trillion dollars down to about eight-fifty.

I didn't really want to tackle this now but knew I had to get started. The first one in the phone book was AAA Storage. They didn't have a warehouse rented to Ducky Nash and the lady asked me why wasn't I in school.

TEN

I don't know if it happens this way where you live, but the Spring sky here is really extraordinary. At the horizon it's nearly white with just a hint of palest blue mixed in. Then there's a layer of pale blue with just a touch of white. Then the blue gets darker in the next layer, and the next, until directly overhead is a wide swath of the richest, deepest blue you could imagine, as if the Good Lord had intended all along for us to look skyward from time to time.

It reminds me of one of those color samplers for paint down at the hardware store.

Charlotte and I are walking in Lullwater Park, which is on the campus of Emory University, and a very pretty place even if it is inhabited mostly by rich Yankees come to get an education. Charlotte is holding my hand which makes me very proud, especially since I see a few future tax lawyers giving her the eye.

We stop and sit on a bench by the water and the ducks swim up expecting us to feed them. I'm caught unprepared, but Charlotte has some bread in her purse and begins tossing little pieces out into the water. The ducks eat just like Monroe, but I don't dwell on that, because I'm watching her do this thing and wondering why I am so lucky to have such a vision give me her love.

Her hair sparkles white in the sunlight, roots and all, and her face is virtually unblemished by time or wear. Her lips are pursed slightly in concentration and it's all I can do to keep from flinging myself at her and begging her to never leave me.

"Jimmy," she says after a moment.

"Hmmm."

"It's time."

"Time for what?"

"I've still got an egg left."

I have to admit this surprises me. "You can tell that, can you?"

"Uh-huh. I can feel that little sucker getting ready to hunker down."

"Do you want to go home?"

"I don't want to do it at home."

"Do you want to just jump in the bushes?"

"I want it to be somewhere special. I was thinking of the Ritz-Carlton. Maybe we could order some room service if it wouldn't be too much money."

This cuts me a little. "Jesus, Charlotte. I got money."

"I know. But I was thinking that if we start doing what we're going there to do it might not get all eaten."

And that is how we came to be on the eighth floor of the Atlanta Ritz-Carlton. Why I made the bellman close the drapes as tight as they're ever likely to be closed with me standing a good twenty feet away is another story.

After the Great JuJube Incident, Petey and I never were that close. We didn't have a falling out or anything, we just sort of drifted apart.

But one night around Christmas that year Petey calls me out of the blue and invites me to spend the night. So I do. And I come to find out that the main reason he wanted me to spend the night was so that we could sneak up into the belltower of the Methodist Church his parents belonged to.

They were having what they called The Living Nativity that year, which meant that folks dressed like Wise Men and a shepherd or two stood out on the front lawn of the church with an old wooden backstop behind them and a spotlight out front, and pretended to be humble...

...while me and Petey saw who could hawk the biggest pearl, which is vulgar, I know, but that was the nature of our association, for distance and accuracy.

It wasn't that hard. Back in those days bubble gum only cost a penny and you got your money's worth. After working up four or five pieces I could nearly hit the street. Petey was homed-in on his Aunt Wilma, who was playing Mary that year, but couldn't clear the backstop.

We were a good hundred feet off the ground but that wasn't the problem. The problem was that the wind conditions made it almost impossible to judge. Petey finally cleared the backstop only to whack the Baby Jesus and then asked me if I really believed in Hell. I let go a gem that would've made Bobby Knight proud only to see a gust of wind catch it about the same time Reverend Grace, which I swear to God was his real name, walk down the front steps and get smeared right on the back of the head, which as genetics would have it didn't have hardly any hair left at all.

Since the gum I was chewing was grape, he naturally assumed the problem was pigeons. So he went inside and turned on the carillon, which wasn't really bells but some electronic facsimile, at about five million decibels in the hope of driving the imaginary varmints away, but which instead only succeeded in causing me to lose my balance until I found myself hanging upside-down over the rail with Petey's grip on my sneaker the only thing between me and the manger.

To this day I have a terrible fear of heights. I don't much like *Silent Night* any more, either.

Charlotte comes to bed wearing a pale green nightie that looks like a workout suit for Playboy Bunnies. What happened after that I'm not saying, specifically, I mean, but trust me when I say that if it ever happened to you you'd just roll over and want somebody to scratch your belly.

I'm nearly asleep when Charlotte gets up and goes into the bathroom. This in itself is not unusual except that I hear her clamoring around in there like a left-handed bartender. So I get up to investigate, since I am duly licensed to do that very thing.

I do not approve of nor adhere to stereotypes of any kind, gender-related or otherwise. Such things diminish all humanity and separate us from the God within us. But—there are absolutely three things a man does not do to a woman even if she is Hell-bent on bearing his offspring.

1) Never make eye-contact with a woman's hair when she first wakes up. No matter how much you love her the expression on your face will make her think you don't.

2) Never watch her get dressed, especially the pantyhose. If you like it she'll think you're a pervert, and if you don't she'll think you don't love her.

3) And I saved the most important for last...Never, ever, in this or any other millennia, EVER follow a woman into the bathroom. Frankly, I'd rather not say why except that you'll just have to trust me.

She'd left the door ajar and I see her in there with some contraption that looks like a miniature version of the chemistry set I got the Christmas I turned nine. Monroe found out that you could mix baking soda with some of the chemicals and create a concoction that if fed to chickens would make them explode right before your eyes.

Naturally I have it taken away from me before New Years' and Monroe offers as his way of apologizing,

"Boy, Mama and Daddy sure are sensitive, ain't they?"

I'm not about to violate the Third Great Law, so I stand there until I can't take it any more and clear my throat.

Charlotte jumps like I just goosed her and gives me an eye so mean that I scoot back a step, which she has only done three other times, and which you might've already guessed is how the Three Great Laws came into being.

"Honey, what are you doing in there?" And believe me

I'm as civil as a rookie priest.

"You need to use the facilities?" she asks, and if the tone of her voice was a gun I'd be ducking about now.

"No, ma'am."

"Then git."

I know I should leave well enough alone but I do think all men carry this gene which won't allow it.

"Are you sick?"

She shakes her head and blows a stream through her nose that if I wasn't looking right at her I'd swear it was a bull.

"No. If you must know, Mr. Nosey Britches, I'm taking a pregnancy test."

I call upon every ounce of my earthly powers not to laugh, knowing that if I do I might as well join the Brothers at St. Paul's and stomp grapes full-time.

"Charlotte," I say gently. "It's only been twenty minutes. I don't think it's supposed to work that fast."

"So when did you become such an expert on the reproductive process? Which it may be awhile before you become familiar with again, if you take my meaning."

I do a Bob Beamon into bed and pray that I can fall asleep before she gets back. After a little bit I hear her and squeeze my eyes and try to unfold myself from the tight little ball I've worked myself into.

And then, in a way that will amaze me until they finally scatter my molecules to the four winds, now and forever more, she snuggles up to me as though no evil will ever pass between us.

"It didn't take," she whispers. "Reckon we should try again.

The next day I use all my vast deductive insights and come to the conclusion that if the wrongfully appropriated materials are being moved in on Monday, then there's a good chance that they might be moved out on a Monday, too, since there's no one there to watch them.

Since this is Monday I hit the road about two a.m. Only tonight I'm prepared. I'm dressed in my Pierre Cardin jogging suit, as if we could possibly believe he did much jogging, but which Charlotte, ma belle chere, gave me for my birthday last year, I am in Mrs. Bocook's Nash, which would only attract attention if you were a weird-car buff or a lovesick terrapin, and even if you were the latter you still might be daunted by the size, and I have a thermos of coffee and two peanut butter sandwiches.

The jelly is muscadine and Charlotte made it herself. I keep a jar of Smucker's strawberry preserves stashed in my van for such emergencies, and I scrape off Charlotte's jelly and put on my own. I would let Dumb Eddie ride me piggy-back before ever doing anything to deliberately hurt her feelings, so I'm trying to work out some kind of allergic reaction for when the last of this batch is gone.

Baby powder gives me a bad rash, go figure, so when we're down to the last jar I'm going to layer on the baby powder until I look like Case Study #412 at the Clearasil Labs.

"Good Lord, Jimmy, what happened to you?"

"I don't know, Charlotte, honey, it must be the muscadine jelly."

"And that's your favorite, too."

"Ain't that the way it always is."

I cruise by the entrance to the warehouse and am so delighted to see the same guy standing guard out there that I spill some coffee in my lap, and if you've ever had it happen you know exactly how unpleasant it can be.

I park at the sainted chiropractor's lot because I don't need to see the Fireman's Drag Races again even if Chris Berman is there doing live play-by-play. All I have to do is wait.

It's forty-five minutes and halfway through my second sandwich, which I realize shows a God-awful lack of restraint on my part, when I see the truck pull out. This time there are no markings at all. It's what Yankees would call non-descript and we would call plain as your granny.

Then I see the Olds pull out right behind it and my stomach does a little tumble. Or at least it would if it wasn't stuck together with peanut butter. It means that Lee Sharpley is not checking on his parolees or even taking a little kickback. He's in this thing way past his chin.

I catch a piece of luck when a truck from the Atlanta Journal comes by and falls in behind the truck-Olds convoy. I pull out right behind the truck to give myself some cover.

The convoy picks up I-85 North toward the South Carolina border, which is actually east of us but I didn't have any thing to do with assigning Interstate directions. They must've given that job to a retired I.R.S. agent. I lose my cover about five miles along, but lag far enough behind so that I catch the draft of a semi hauling Busch Beer, pardon the pun, but which is very comforting to know that he's on the job so early, and then cruise along all nondescript like it's nobody's business.

Except that we travel for two hours and nothing has happened yet. Another half hour or so and we'll be in South Carolina, and if it comes to that I might stop on my way back and buy some fireworks. The cigarettes are cheaper, too, but since I don't smoke and discourage anybody I know who does, I'll have to make do with some M-80's.

I do flash on Tukey Watson, though.

Tukey was a guy I learned about my first year under cover. Tukey would drive to North Carolina and pick up a load of cigarettes, which he could get for about sixty cents a pack wholesale, and then sell them on the street for a buck a pack, which was still a lot less than you could buy them in stores since Georgia taxes cigarettes out the wahzoo.

Tukey had his own route, too, and I've got to admit that it was a marvel. He was the only door-to-door illegal cigarette man I ever knew. He would just walk down the streets and folks would holler out their windows like he was Willy Wonka.

"Heave me a coupla packs of Winstons, Tukey."

"Yes, ma'am."

And he'd toss them from one of those big canvas bags

like paper boys use.

People would stop their cars dead in the middle of the street.

"What can you do for me on a carton of Salems, Tukey?"

"Ten dollars today, sir. But if you buy two cartons I'll throw in a bonus pack for the twenty."

It wasn't long before Tukey was moving about three hundred cartons a week, which by my calculations put him in the same tax bracket as the Governor. Only he didn't pay taxes on his income, which you may not know but are required to do even on ill-gotten gains (and if you're up on your television you know is how we finally put the quietus to Al Capone).

But the thing that got to me was that he was unloading about fifty cartons a week to kids.

So I had him zapped and he got off with probation and a stiff fine. The last I heard he was working the same scam somewhere in Florida, who I hear taxes cigarettes even worse than we do on account of all the tourists who come to visit and are trapped down there. And when they get withdrawal they're too far from the border to do anything about it, so they spring for the full price and pretend that they're still having a good time.

I'm still thinking about Tukey when I see the convoy pull into the first South Carolina Welcome Station. There's not a fireworks stand in sight, so naturally I'm a little disappointed. Then again, maybe it's just as well since the last time I bought fireworks Monroe grabbed them all, tied them into a bundle, and torched it in one get-go. One of Daddy's goats still has the hiccups.

There's nobody at the station except a couple of truckers catching a few winks and some people from Illinois who had to give the kids an overdose of Tylenol to settle them down and are now letting them sleep it off.

The truck pulls up and Dumb Eddie gets out. The Olds pulls up and Lee Sharpley gets out with Slick riding shotgun. There is a Lincoln that at first I think is a tourist until I see the guy get out and walk up to Lee. He's got company, too, and his sidekick is even less to brag about than Slick. He's tall and dumpy and looks like Alfred E. Neuman with a beer gut.

Alfred takes the keys, Mr. Lincoln hands Lee a briefcase, which we all know contains the loot unless it's Dumb Eddie's supper. They handshake all around like good Baptists and Lee, Slick and Dumb Eddie drive off, except that now the Olds is dragging a mite and shooting sparks at the speed bumps.

I let Lee take the lead. I don't need to see them divide up the money to know that they each get a cut. Maybe I should call Penney's and warn them that Dumb Eddie's on his way, though. They might want to break out the Christmas catalogue a little early.

I do sneak a little peek, which is formidable in a Nash, and time it so that I pass the Lincoln just as everybody is getting in and won't even notice me unless one of them is a weird-car buff or a lovesick terrapin.

The car has Florida plates and I get the number.

If things weren't so all-fired serious I'd stop and ask them if they knew Tukey Watson.

ELEVEN

I oversleep, which I hardly ever do, and am late for work. Not to mention that I'm just a little bit grouchy. So it seems only natural that I have a note on my desk from my boss asking me to step into his office when I get in.

On my way I'm thinking of things to say to him even if I probably won't.

"Did you forget your umbrella, or did somebody mistake you for a walrus and chunk you back into the pit?"

Or

"Did you miss a spot on your chin when you shaved this morning, or is that the tip of the heifer's tail you tried to swallow whole?"

Instead I stick my head in his doorway and say, "Yes, sir?", then smile like a new convert.

"Sit down, Jim," he says, and it scares me a little for him to be so formal. I'm thinking I might've gotten transferred to Omaha and he's trying to break it to me gently.

"I was going through your records and noticed that your receipts were down a little last month."

It sounds like he thinks the temptation finally got me and I don't know whether to be piqued or just slap him one. In my entire career I have embezzled exactly fifty cents, and that was July two years ago when we were having a heat wave and I bought a can of pop at Toby's and forgot to put the money back. So sue me. I could probably get Al Katz to claim I was delirious and finagle me a Worker's Comp claim out of it.

I play it safe by being direct and mature.

"It turned warm early."

"Pardon?"

"It turned warm early. Business is always up, so to speak, during the cold weather because some folks got little else to do. It always slacks off when it first turns warm and then picks up again when people have had their fill of fresh air. I think you'll see it pick back up this month."

"I see," he says. And then he pauses like he's got something caught in his throat. I'm thinking I might have to move in to do a Heimlich, and wouldn't that be a challenge, first to get my arms all the way around him and second, if the whole ass-end of that heifer popped out.

Then he goes on, thank the Lord.

"We'd hate to have anything happen to your work."

He sounds sincere and that baffles me. "Sir?"

"It seems that your efforts have come to the attention of some very important people in Washington. In fact, they've inquired about your participation in some efficiency studies."

"You mean the I.R.S. is thinking about getting into the condom business in a big way?"

He does a little shiver, and all I can say is that you should be glad you're not here to see it.

"Well, no, not exactly. But apparently some of our other operations on a similar scale are not very profitable. And Washington wants to see if they couldn't be more so."

Well dye me brown and call me a gopher. What a Hell of a note this is.

"I'd do whatever I could to help, sir," I say.

"Of course our primary function is to root out violators."

"Of course."

"And we wouldn't want to do anything else that might compromise our work."

"But if we manage to double-dip a little in the process that's okay by Uncle Sam."

"Well...yes, in a manner of speaking."

What could I say? "Just let me know what I can do," I say, getting up.

"I'll keep you posted," he answers, and nods toward the

door.

And as I'm walking down the hallway I almost laugh out loud, and would even if I wasn't suffering from sleep deprivation. The Government is so stupendously screwed up and in debt that It'd just as soon sell condoms as collect taxes as long as the payroll was being met.

Come to think about it, a few machines on Capitol Hill and The Pentagon would probably make them self-sufficient.

Maybe I ought to check into getting the hot dog concession at Falcons games. We could have our own I.R.S. nicknames, too. Call the foot long the *Before Dog* and the regular hot dog the *After Dog*.

I get a line on Mr. Lincoln's plates and it turns out that his name is Henry Bennett and he's from Jacksonville, Florida. He's in sales and doing fairly well, even without dealing in stolen goods. He's a family man and his taxes are done by a professional. He's been audited twice and passed with flying colors both times.

I couldn't begin to guess how he's laundering his money without following him around and Charlotte would never stand for that.

Except that I remember there's a greyhound racing track near Jacksonville and maybe I could tell her we're going to St. Augustine and accidentally get lost.

The only thing that jumps out at me is that he moved to Florida four years ago from Columbus, Ohio, which is the home town of Lee Sharpley's alma mater. I don't know for sure, but it'd be a safe bet that it's old Hank's alma mater, too. Now I know for sure why I never liked Woody Hayes.

I do some quick checking on Lee. He's single, lives in a little townhouse and files the short form. As far as the government is concerned he's just another hard-working public servant. I don't know how he's laundering his money either, except maybe for socks.

Eric Tannenbaum has got me puzzled. I've got no idea if he's involved in this or just another unfortunate business owner with hanky-panky going on under his nose. What I do know is that he is way the other side of well off.

Besides City Delivery he owns a big restaurant, a couple of fast food franchises, a temporary employment agency and a cleaning service. He pulls in a million dollars a year and his net worth is at least five times that.

And he keeps a low profile. None of those social organizations or G.O.P. dinners where the well-heeled go to pat each other on the back for being such outstanding citizens. Even his businesses are operated through a law firm.

So the only thing left for me to do is call my invisible dispatcher friend out at City Delivery.

She answers on the first ring.

"Could I speak to Mr. Tannenbaum, please?"

"Who?"

"Eric Tannenbaum. We used to play golf together at Princeton."

"Fine by me. Except he don't work here."

"He's the owner."

"Oh. Well, if he's that, it's news to me, Bub." Then I hear her thinking to herself. "Hey, is this the same guy who called in here to say his dog was wandering around our premises—"

Click. I hated to do it but there was no place for me to go with it.

I called all the other companies Eric owns and nobody there had ever heard of him either. The lady who ran the cleaning service said that she was hired by some dink in a three-piece suit downtown, and didn't really care about the rest as long as she got her paycheck on time.

I also know that I have first-hand knowledge of about a jillion felonies and can't sit on that information forever, Ducky or not. I hate to admit it, but I'm intrigued by the intrigue now and want to see it through.

So I call a buddy of mine at the F.B.I. to do a little informal snooping. We're able to talk to each other without doing a lot of explaining since we're both in the same boat, more or less.

I'd also like to find out about putting some machines in all the F.B.I. bathrooms.

But when I casually mention truck hijackings he acts like I'm a Schnauzer that just stuck its nose in his crotch.

"What's your interest?"

"Just some scuttlebutt," I say innocently. "Why?"

"Because, my bud, we're really up against it. If this was rain it'd be a monsoon. If this was snow it'd be a blizzard. If this was cowshit it'd be Oklahoma."

"I get the picture. What's the dope?"

Then he lowers his voice like we were in high school and he'd just found his Daddy's cache of Playboys.

"We're talking over a hundred in the last four years. Fifty just in the last year-and-a-half. And whoever is doing it is well organized. Some of the drivers just stop long enough to take a crap and when they come out their rigs are gone."

"And you don't know who's behind it?"

"We know that they all occurred within a hundred and fifty mile radius of Atlanta. Beyond that, we might as well be morons. So tell me about this scuttlebutt."

"Just loose talk," I say nonchalantly. "Stuff about T.V.'s and stereos and things like that."

"Well, that's it and that's it."

"What?"

"The talk may be loose but right on the money. And it's all consumer-grade stuff like that. Easy to fence and impossible to trace. Hell, they even took a load of hot tubs if you can imagine that."

"That is strange. Well, gotta go—"

"Hey, wait Jimmy. You know anything about this you gotta let me in on it. The heat on my hiney is unbearable and I'm just third-string."

"If I come across anything solid you'll be the first to know."

"Okay. Thanks."

I hang up hoping that crossing your eyes when you tell a whopper accounts for something on the cosmic balance sheet.

There wasn't much I didn't already know, except that the four-year period made the loop. That was about the time old Hank Bennett moved to Florida. And the increase in frequency seemed to tie-in with Slick and the gang coming to work at City Delivery.

I've still got that damn key in my pocket, too, and it's beginning to burn my thigh. I'm starting to feel that I really don't owe Ducky a thing, but deep down I know. He deserved better.

So I call through all the A's, B's and C's in the Yellow Pages and get zip, except for one lady who asks me what would Donald Duck be doing renting a warehouse here in Atlanta.

I finally decide that I need a change of scenery.

Buckhead is to Atlanta what Bel-Air is to Los Angeles, and every city has its own. In Decatur it's the Laurel Community where Mrs. Bocook lives, and myself by association, except that it's ancient and most of the people have kept their properties intact so that you could fire off a howitzer in the middle of the night and your neighbors wouldn't even hear it. And if they did they'd probably just think it was General Sherman coming back through and hide in the cellar.

Buckhead has a lot of gates, hedges and circular drive ways. And if Uncle Sam ever turned me loose up there I could probably find enough funny business to wipe out this year's deficit, except that about half of Buckhead is tax lawyers.

It's a pretty drive, though, and I enjoy it. All the lawns are perfect and all the houses look dignified and serene. There are a couple who haven't taken the hint yet and have those little jockeys on the lawn that look like Bojangles Robinson. Then there are the sincere who just don't get it and have painted over the faces of their jockeys until they look like Mr. Bill with a tan.

I find the residence of one Eric Tannenbaum and park down the street. I don't expect him to be there, but I thought that if I just stared at his house long enough, and pretended it was a computer, a clue might jump out at me, or else somebody will come up and ask me my business and maybe I'll at least get a peek at him right before they cart me off.

I don't judge by appearances but I trust my instincts. And I can spot a phoney clear down the block.

He has one of those houses which somebody who should know better told him was Tudor, but which instead looks like an overgrown gingerbread house. I stare for awhile until I think that any minute an old witch is going to come tearing out the front door after a couple of little fat kids, and I know it's time for another nap.

There's a blue Volvo in the driveway and I think the Missus is probably in. If that sounds sexist, I'm sorry, but there you have it. Since I'm in my van and work clothes I might be able to scam it.

"Hi, I'm Jim. I'm here to fix the jacuzzi."

"Yeah, it has been acting up lately."

"Here's your trouble, ma'am. Olive pits in the drain. You might think about using pimento from now on."

"Thank you. I'll tell Eric when he gets home."

"Okay. And since we're on the subject, do you reckon he knows that a major hijacking ring is operating out of one of his warehouses?"

I pull up to the house and get out. So far, so good. No Pinkerton's, no attack dogs, no loud noises. So I knock on the door.

A lady comes to the door and I know immediately that she wouldn't buy any if I was The Pope handing out silver dollars. She's got a hard look about her that tells me she'd probably been pretty once but had done things to get that close to money she'd never really been proud of, but which had gotten her into the Junior League and a shrink to explain it all to her, and was probably doing a little flirting with her golf pro just to get even.

She's dressed in a pantsuit with gold baubles at the ear and wrist that probably cost more than my entire wardrobe. Her hair and makeup had been done by professionals.

"Mrs. Tannenbaum?" I ask, and you'd have thought I'd just come from confession. "I'm sorry to bother you but I'm looking for some people by the name of Cushing and seem to have gotten lost."

"How'd you know who I was?" she asks, and if you poured scalding water down her throat it'd be ice before it hit bottom.

"I stopped a coupla houses back and they said that you were nice and might be able to help me."

"That's because they think we're Jewish," she says, and smiles a little at that. I smile back and we both know that ages ago when things were different we might've grown up together. "Look, I don't know anybody named Cushing but you can try the next street over."

I nod and take my leave and she goes back inside. I glance to see if she's watching after me but all the drapes stay put, so I dawdle just long enough to see if anybody else takes an interest.

I get in my van and pull away. Maybe I could go back and tell her I'm the Jacuzzi man after all and while I was there could I please look for some clues. Maybe she would believe me if I told her I was the olive man and was there to service her wet bar. Maybe she would believe me if I told her I was lost and would she help me find my mommy. All I know is that if there's a clue somewhere's around it would just about have to bite me on the batoom for me to see it.

And Hoo-diddly-doo, watch those chompers!

I no sooner made the circle and started back when I see the car pull into the driveway. It's a new Olds and I've seen it before. So have you.

It's broad daylight and there's no place for me to hide, so I can only drive by and then stop next door in the hope of spying a little.

The people next door are on alert. I see drapes parting in six different windows on all three floors.

"*Who is that?*"

"*I don't know. Maybe it's the Jacuzzi man.*"

"*I told you we should've switched to onions.*"

It doesn't matter. I see that it's Lee Sharpley dressed in his

Sunday best, and he goes right up like he owns the place.

I drive off thinking I have two possibilities. Either Mr. Tannenbaum is behind the whole thing and Lee is his number one flunky, or else Lee is paying his respects to Mrs. Tannenbaum in a way that Mr. Tannenbaum probably wouldn't find all that respectful. Or maybe both.

Or they could be cousins, who's to say?

TWELVE

I get up at five the next morning just so I can cruise by the Tannenbaum's on my way into town. Sharpley's Olds is still there and Mr. Tannenbaum doesn't seem to be, so I know that I haven't really missed anything except what has been going on indoors, which is something that really doesn't interest me anyway. Lee reminds me of a gobbler hen that's all neck and legs, and the thought of him in some amorous situation makes my orange juice back up on me.

Once that passes I start in on my sausage and egg biscuit. I'm making a mess, too, but that's not the point. I'm wondering what we did before all these fast food places started making this stuff.

Mama always made breakfast, even after one of Monroe's teachers sent home a note that said she thought it made him doze off in class, and belch in his sleep besides. In college I stopped eating breakfast altogether, which is a bad habit, I know, but since I had basketball practice every afternoon I had to take an eight o'clock class just to get all my schoolwork in.

One time we were having a cold spell and I was running late, so I had to hop right out of the shower onto the pavement. My hair was still a little damp, and when I sat down in class I noticed that everybody was watching me. Then I noticed that every time I moved there would be this tinkling sound.

Turned out it was ice. My hair had frozen. It took me fifteen minutes to comb all the ice out of my hair and I caught a bad cold.

My basketball coach was less than sympathetic.

"You goofing off, Nance?"

"Doe, sir."

"Then what's your problem?"

"Dust a little code, sir."

"A cold? You ever hear of Jerry West or Elgin Baylor letting a little cold get in the way?"

"Doe, sir."

"Then give me twenty laps. And stop that damned hackin'!"

One of the greatest benefits to humanity that came out of the Women's Movement is blow dryers. Before the Movement most men would have been out-and-out ashamed to use one. One of my girlfriends in college had one of those little portable dryers that amounted to putting a rubber bag over your head and cranking up the volume. I wonder what my coach would've thought if he'd seen me in that get-up.

Now it is so commonplace that some blow dryers even have jacks to use in the car. I've seen guys on the road with a carphone in one ear and a blow dryer in the other. How they steer is one of the last great mysteries of the twentieth century.

I've got a blow dryer, too. I just don't use it in public. Charlotte likes to dry my hair for me when we have time. She thinks it helps us bond. She got playful one time and stuck it down my shorts. I got all red-faced and she quit. You think I'd tell her I liked it?

Lee comes out a little after seven dressed like an Episcopalian but in an entirely different suit than the night before, and as innocent as a pup. This I can't figure. Why would he bother to dress so nicely? I'm also thinking that he and Mrs. Tannenbaum have one Hell of an arrangement.

Then she comes out, too. Nothing wrong here, folks. Just the guy who's helping my husband loot half the Eastern Seaboard and keeping the toilet seat limber while he's away.

And they kiss! Right on the mouth and right there in front of me, the people next door and Bojangles Robinson. I guess when you live in Buckhead you can pick and choose what appearances you want to maintain.

I decide to follow him. Once we leave Buckhead we're in rush hour traffic and there are too many cars for him to notice me.

I think the driving rules for Atlanta are a little different than other places. Whenever a child in Atlanta comes of age he or she must take Georgia Driver's Education. The handbook alone is over a hundred pages, and very thorough.

Here's a sampling of some of the chapter headings:

Chapter Four—How to Occupy Two Lanes by Straddling the Center Line

Chapter Six—How to Cruise the Passing Lane at Forty Miles-per-Hour and Ignore all the Horns and Gestures

Chapter Seven—How to Know When Your Brakes Are Just Bad Enough to Maim but not Kill

Chapter Nine—How to Cut Somebody Off When Changing Lanes so That if They Hit You it will be Their Fault

And my personal favorite...

Chapter Twelve—How to Cut Across Four Lanes of Traffic and Still Make the Exit You Just Passed

There are chapters in proper etiquette, too. Such as *The Proper Use of the Georgia Peace Sign*, which in case you didn't know utilizes just one finger, and *The Proper Use of the Georgia Credit Card*, which is a very valuable emergency procedure.

The Georgia Credit Card is a short piece of garden hose and a milk jug. Together they are used to siphon gasoline out of somebody else's tank, usually without troubling them with details. Trucks usually work best since the gas tank is already elevated and you don't have to suck so hard.

One time Monroe was invited to Amy Tollison's Sweet Sixteen birthday party because she had told him that once she turned sixteen her Mama would let her car-date. Monroe is like the cock-of-the-walk until he discovers that Amy has just had a mouthful of braces installed.

"It ain't just the pain," he said later. "It's that whistling sound she makes."

Monroe was driving an old beat-up Ford Daddy let him use because if he tore it up it wouldn't be any great loss. And the thing just drank gas. So naturally he couldn't resist a whole yardful of cars just asking for it. It'd help cut his losses with Amy, too.

He took his Credit Card out of his trunk and started making the rounds. He'd already racked up about eight gallons when he came to Shangri-La, Mrs. Tollison's Roadmaster, which had about a fifty-gallon tank.

I have to give him his due, Monroe was a master of the Credit Card. He had the lungs of a jackass and could usually get it going the first hit. Once you've got suction then all you have to do is hold the hose. He puffed a couple of times and then let it rip.

Except that right in the middle of his inhale Amy comes out on the porch looking for him.

"Monroe? Monroe, honey, it's time for the cake!"

And Monroe gets a mouthful of Sunoco Premium and has got no place to spit without alerting Amy to his whereabouts. He just has to wait her out, holding about a pint of gas in his mouth until she finally gives up and goes back inside. By the time she does and he gets to spit the inside of his mouth is burning so bad he can't breathe and smells like a truck stop.

He goes inside and heads straight for the punchbowl, when Amy grabs his arm and pulls him toward the cake. Which is covered with sixteen candles and one in the middle carved into the number '16' that beats the Washington Monument all to pieces, and it all looks like High Mass.

Monroe might've graduated eighty-second out of eighty three in his class (Ebie Sherman dropped out in February to get married but still had enough credits to graduate), but he did know that fire and gasoline don't mix.

But Amy is persistent.

"Monroe, help me blow the candles out," she purrs.

"Mfff, mfff," he says, which is about all he can manage with his mouth closed.

"Oh, Monroe, honey, don't be silly," she coos, slaps him on the arm, and leans him toward the cake with her. "On three, now. Ready. One...two...three!"......

I don't know if you've ever seen a fire eater at the carnival, but it's the same principle. Monroe blew fire twenty-five feet across the room. It even seemed to spread as it went, taking out a lampshade, some drapes, the backend of Amy's Cocker Spaniel 'Lulu', Mrs. Tollison's favorite pillow, which came from the Bicentennial and had 'America 1776-1976' embroidered on it, and Larry Albert's hair, which was red and curly and the pride of his life.

Everybody was in shock for a second and then just stared from Monroe, to the room, most of which still crackled, to Monroe again. Thinking quick he covers his mouth with his hand.

"Excuse me," he says. "Must've been the pizza."

There are also separate lines at the Highway Department for people who have just moved here and need to get a new driver's license. The express line is for people from Ohio, Michigan, Illinois, New York and any part of Canada, since they already know our ways. The other line is for everybody else and they have to take the test.

It's not long before I realize that Lee is heading home. On the way I roll numbers over in my head. It's a bad habit, but after all I am an accountant, even if you couldn't swear to it by looking at me.

Fifty trucks in eighteen months. Bennett's been in Florida four years. That's probably a hundred and fifty trucks. A truck would carry a couple hundred televisions or VCR's, each with a fence value of maybe a hundred bucks a pop. That's twenty thousand dollars a truck times one hundred fifty trucks is...three million dollars. Whoa. And who knows what hot tubs bring these days.

Maybe Lee even has all his fraternity brothers working franchises somewhere.

He pulls up to his apartment and gets out. I park at a Starvin' Marvin across the street. It's about twenty minutes before he comes out again, this time dressed down, the way I've always seen him at work. And he doesn't take the Olds. Instead he takes a two year-old Chevy Lumina.

Oddlier and oddlier. Why the uptown duds just to drive home? Maybe it's Mrs. Tannenbaum who's the real Czarina of this operation. Maybe they play 'boss and secretary' when nobody's looking. Maybe Lee told her he runs I.B.M. Maybe it's a Buckhead community ordinance.

So where does Mr. Tannenbaum fit into all this? And where is Mr. Tannenbaum? Is he in The Bahamas running things from afar and sitting on all the loot? Is he buried in the back yard? Is he in a home somewhere and Lee is taking advantage of one of his businesses and Mrs. Tannenbaum to boot?

Maybe I should get Jim Earl to write me a song.

Oh, Mr. Tannenbaum, please call home
This sure ain't the time for you to roam
Your wife's got your money
And it ain't so funny
That she's also taken up with an Uncle Tim gnome
Named Lee
Sharp-ley
Whooey, pe-tooie
Sharp-ley...

I've got a headache and machines to tend to.

Snuff Waldrep's Bar-B-Q is the exact opposite of Rudy's. I'd use the word antithesis but you'd probably think I was taking on. The place is dirty, ugly, smelly, and if Mrs. Waldrep is working the counter you might have to eat facing the street.

Snuff's specialty is hash. Hash is a distinctly Southern

delicacy, maybe because we're a trusting lot and will eat stuff that tastes good even if we can't tell what it is by looking at it.

Essentially, hash is...well, hash. It's almost as if somebody decided to clean out the refrigerator, chop the remains into fine little pieces in case some of it has lost its shape, and cook it all together. Snuff has an entire grill that's about two feet by two feet devoted to it.

Every kind of meat imaginable, but predominantly pork and beef, the parts of which you don't want to know, trust me, with the occasional smidge of chicken, turkey, goat and whatever thrown in, is chopped up into slivers, piled high in the middle of this grill, spiced and double-spiced, salted enough to throw your blood pressure into high gear, and finally covered in Snuff's special sauce, which is the real secret.

Then it's served over rice in what looks like a big cone so that you can eat it on the run if you have to. And believe me, a day or so later you'll have to.

It's an acquired taste and you need to work into it gradually. I never eat the stuff. I hardly ever eat in Snuff's at all ever since I heard a Health Inspector swear that a wayward mouse once tried to hotfoot it across the grill and was never seen again. Sometimes I have the short ribs, but at least you can still see all the body parts it's made from.

I've helped Snuff a couple of times with the Health Department, who couldn't keep him closed down even if they wanted to on account of the whole town would riot, and he has six machines in his bathrooms that do a good business.

His facilities are disgusting, though, and I hate to go in there. The floor is always sticky and reminds me of Saturday nights at the old Avalon Theatre. And the plumbing is always broke.

Once he even drilled a little hole in the wall at floor level, but swore up-and-down that it was intended strictly for ventilation and not for the purposes guys were using it.

The lunch crowd is just starting to file in and so I just nod my greeting and wave to Snuff on my way back. He gets this pained expression on his face like there's something he needs to talk to me about, but a customer distracts him and I'm not sure I want to know until I have to, anyway.

Mrs. Waldrep is working behind the counter and I hear a couple of people whisper something about Mr. Ed before they move on down to a table.

I see it the minute I walk into the men's room. Somebody has taken one of my dark green Regulars, in toto regalia, which by the way is a very pretty color, and skewered it with an ice pick right into the heart of one of my machines, meaning that I'll have to replace it. There is also a note attached, and I pull out a pair of gloves just to be on the safe side.

Here hangs the ghost of Reggie Moore
We was buddies once before
'til I catch him sneakin' out my door
Now there ain't no Reggie no more.

Maybe Jim Earl ought to ride with me for awhile.

Charlotte's in the kitchen making spaghetti for supper, and I'm so glad to see her that I pick her up and squeeze her, and then set her down on a burner she'd been using to boil water and only turned off a couple of minutes before, accidentally burning her butt.

She bops me one and then feels so guilty that she lets me put some cream on her wounded area under the general premise that she couldn't adequately reach the spot. I would never speak out of turn about any of Charlotte's private things, but if there is a reason why some people respond to certain parts of other people's anatomies other than their own animalistic natures, then I thank the Good Lord for plugging Charlotte and me into the same extension cord.

"Jimmy."

"Hmmm."

"Are you rubbin' for medicinal purposes or are you rubbin' for fun?"

"Well, another little daub won't hurt," I say.

"I'm not pregnant this time," she says, and I know she's serious. I also know that I have to back off and let her fix her pants or I won't stand a fly's chance in Rudy's of concentrating on what she needs to tell me, which I know would hurt her feelings.

"It's plain discouraging," she says.

I hold her in a way that I don't have to very often, but would do every day if I had to because it makes me feel necessary and important.

"It takes time, honey. Sometimes months."

"You know, I've been thinkin'."

"What?"

"Maybe the real reason I want this baby so bad is because Mama was so poor at it, bless her heart."

"You have unrequited feelings," I whisper. "Believe me, I know what that's like. But I also know that when people get hurt real bad in this world they either become takers or givers. And you are a giver of the best kind. So naturally you would want to give something back that would enrich the world in a way that you never got."

And then I feel her trembling a little on my neck and it scares me. In the whole time I've known her I've only seen her cry twice, and that was when the Braves lost the World Series in 1991 and 1992.

"I love you with all my heart," I say. "I thank God for you every day. And I know that you're going to be one Hell of a mama."

"Jimmy Nance," she says. "You are the joy and sorrow of my life."

"And don't I know it," I answer.

We're very quiet that night, and I don't know what it is but I know that things have changed. Not in some dreadful, ominous way, but in a very gentle way you wouldn't even notice if your heart wasn't full to start with.

There is a purpose in life for everyone, and once that purpose is found it buds and blooms and gives off its nectar. And if you're very, very lucky, you find all the new purposes that come with the blossoms so that the purpose will not die. I had the feeling that Charlotte and I were finding some of the new purposes now, and it was very sweet.

I put the radio on while we ate. It's something I hardly ever do. One of the benefits of living in a big town is that there is a radio station for everything. We've got news stations and talk stations and religious stations and even one that broadcasts in Spanish, but which rents itself one morning a week to some people who broadcast in Hindi. We also have a couple called Adult Contemporary. I found one of those. It's only a jump up from elevator music, but it was soft and pleasant and we ate in silence.

After supper I ran Charlotte's bath and cleared the table and did the dishes while she was in it. I went in and washed her back and helped her dry off. I put her in an old flannel nightgown she only wore in the dead of winter, but which was the most comfortable thing she had. And I put her to bed and held her until she fell asleep.

I sat up for awhile thinking about all the stuff going on around me. About how this thing with Lee Sharpley was such a disappointment. Having it good hadn't been enough. He'd gone for the shortcut and I was going to make sure it ended up being the long way around.

That bothered me, too. Wondering if I was doing it just to get even or if I was doing it because it was right. Wondering if there is ever any true justice in a hardened heart, regardless of the motives. And Ducky's key tortured me like Macbeth's dagger.

I hear Charlotte talking in her sleep and I go in and sit beside her. She says 'Mama' once and clutches my hand, so I strip down and get into bed with her. She becomes still again after a moment, and, strangely enough, I find myself at peace.

THIRTEEN

It's Saturday and I decide to make a couple of phone calls from the house just to tie up a few loose ends.

The first was to Mr. Delray, who remembered me right off and didn't seem the least bit bothered that I would call.

"I need to know a little something about the layout of the warehouse," I say, and if you'd heard me you'd think I was from the Salvation Army.

"Shoot," he answers, which if he knew just how bad a shot I was he'd never even consider such a thing.

"I need to know if there are places where stuff could be stashed for maybe up to a week without arousing suspicion."

There is a pause which makes me think that he's either worried about me or else that I've got an in with Madame Ruth, who is a palmist out back of Conyers.

"I thought that might have something to do with it. They got a second floor out there. Only it don't go all the way across. It's sort of like a loft, if you know what I mean."

To tell him I did because I lived in such a place would have been redundant and obtuse. So instead I say,

"Yeah?"

"There are two stairways to it and they're always locked. There's a freight elevator to it and it's always locked. And if you get anywhere near it The Wild Bunch give you the death look."

I think about the key. "Padlocked?"

"No. Heavy-duty door locks."

Manure. Back to the Yellow Pages.

"So what does everyone say is up there?"

"Unclaimed stuff," he says. "But there's an awful lot of

space for that."

"So who has the key?"

"A guy who they say is some kind of trouble-shooter for the company. Doesn't hit a lick at a snake, though."

"You know his name?"

"Wiry little twerp they call Slick."

I thank him and hang up.

Arnold Carvey, on the other hand, was downright glad to hear from me.

"Got a business proposition for you. You front me the rubbers and I'll just take a little cut."

"Can't do it."

"I thought you'd say that."

"I'd work on the books and that jump shot if I were you."

"Hey, I got overhead."

"Okay, look. I'll give you the number of a wholesaler if you want. Maybe he'll do business with you."

I gave him the number. Think what you want. I'm not sure I did him any harm.

"The reason I called is to see if you could think of anything else about Ducky that might help me."

"Like what?"

"I don't know. He flash any money or do anything out of character for him?"

"Ducky didn't have no character I know about."

"You know what I mean. And don't speak ill of the dead."

He thinks for a minute. "Yeah, he did. One thing."

"What was that?"

"He bought a car."

"Where is it?"

"I ain't got the foggiest."

A car! A car in storage! Eureka! Wait a minute. So what? I sigh. I can't help it. Back to the Yellow Pages.

"Okay, buddy. Thanks."

"How about another dozen or so just to get the market loosened up?"

"I'll think about it."

I hang up thinking that Ducky had a hideout with a car so that he could take it on the lam. (Forgive me, Broderick Crawford). Except that something happened before he could do that. I was getting depressed. Ducky had become the sorrow of my life.

There was only one thing left to do. Take Charlotte to visit my folks. They always hounded me to bring her up, and I had to find a time when I was either so happy that nothing could get me down, or else had nothing left to lose. I figure I'm obligated to take her up there four times a year, just like quarterly reports. I solve this case I'm going to take her up there for a week and then just not show up for the next two years.

My parents really like Charlotte maybe even more than they like me. Mama likes her because she'll sit and listen to her for hours on end, and Daddy likes her because she pulled the greyhound trick with a litter of his coon dogs. He got top price for them, too.

Another reason I don't like to do this is because taking Charlotte anywhere in a car is a real challenge. I love her to death, but the woman cannot go a mile in an automobile without having to use the facilities somewhere. I don't know if it's some deep psychological trauma, or just the hum of the tires on the road, but we can't even go out to eat without stopping at least once. And she gets so self-conscious about it that I'm riding the crest of a guilt trip for the next month.

It reminds me of when my mother used to take Monroe and me to church, and one time in particular.

Daddy went to church exactly fifteen times a year. He would go the first Sunday of every month, to show his respect. Mother's Day, because he loved Mama. Thanksgiving, because we all had things to be thankful for. And Easter, because Mama made him wear a new suit.

I asked him why he didn't go at Christmas and he soured up on me and said that if the Good Lord could see what we'd all done to his birthday He'd roll over in his grave, which isn't exactly Biblical, but I understood his meaning.

Mama, on the other hand, was a stickler for attendance. And every Sunday, rain, sleet or snow, sickness or health, and you could bet your last JuJube that if you had a sudden attack of something on Sunday she'd see right through it, she would cart Monroe and me to church.

Our congregation was small and usually our ministers were, too, since we always seemed to get them on their last legs and just before retirement or death, whichever came first, on account of being such a small congregation we couldn't afford much.

The one that sticks in my mind was Reverend J.D. 'Roadmap' Evans. We called him Roadmap because he was about seventy by the time we got him, and he had preached fire and brimstone so hard for so long that all the blood vessels in his cheeks had burst, and his face, God love him, looked just like the Rand McNally insert of Knoxville.

Mama always sat between Monroe and me as if we'd actually do mischief in the House of God. She always carried a box of Chiclets around in her purse, and if we behaved ourselves we'd get a little treat on the way home. Mama never indulged, even though she had all her real teeth. Maybe she didn't think it was fitting for a grown woman to chew on the Sabbath, I don't know. She never said.

She really didn't have to worry about me or Monroe, either. We both had gotten daydreaming down to an art form. By the time I was eight I could play out an entire basketball game in my head, all the way through one of Roadmap's forty-five minute sermons. And being of a good heart, I shared my secret with Monroe.

So there we'd be every Sunday, still as churchmice while old Roadmap admonished us with the very powers of Doom lest we stumble. I would be moving up court, passing and setting screens and moving down the lane for a layup, while Monroe would be running over offensive linemen to squash the quarterback with his bare hands.

Roadmap even complimented Mama on how well-behaved we both were, though he didn't understand why we would grin sometimes, even inappropriate times, and that when Monroe did it with a little twitch it was downright scary.

One Sunday Monroe took a box of Feen-a-Mint and put all the pieces in Mama's Chiclet box. After church that day Mama said that we had been extra good and would we like a Chiclet?

"No ma'am," Monroe says. And instantly I am suspicious.

"No thank you, Mama," I say, and Monroe is so agitated that I catch on so quickly he shows his teeth at me.

"Well, I think I'll have one," she says, and pops one.

Naturally this catches Monroe by surprise and he slumps back in his seat a little.

We had a big flea market every Sunday in the old Silver Moon Drive-In. They called it a Jockey Lot, don't ask me why. It doesn't exist any more. Like just about every other drive-in in the country, all that's left is broken asphalt, scattered speaker posts and a screen too big to tear down.

"Why don't we go to the Jockey Lot?" Mama says all chipper, meaning that she wants to reward us with a treat and the Jockey Lot is filled with them.

"That's a good idea, Mama," I say, giving Monroe a little wink.

Mama spits her gum out the window and I see Monroe give a sigh of relief, and then I know what he's done. Except that Mama takes another piece out of the box and pops it.

"These things don't hold their flavor long, do they?" she says. "You sure you boys don't want one?"

"No, ma'am," we say in unison.

The Jockey Lot is an amazing and mysterious place, filled with riches beyond your wildest dreams. Sort of like an Arabian Market for white trash.

There are used books and bootleg tapes, eight-track in those days, knives and guns, pots and pans, costume jewelry and baseball cards,closeout clothes and seconds, T-shirts airbrushed on the spot, and food so greasy that had we known about cholesterol back in those days we'd have all just run out into the highway and saved ourselves the trouble.

I used to count all the missing teeth, wishing I had a dollar for every one I saw. I think that was probably the beginning of my accounting career. One time I got all the way up to eight hundred and forty until Mama asks me why I'm staring at everybody's mouth and makes me stop.

There's a guy selling big beach towels with cartoon pictures of semi-naked women on them. Monroe stops to gawk and Mama whacks him in the back of the head. People did that to Monroe so often that by the time he was twelve you could hold a ruler up to the back of his head and it wouldn't bow an inch.

We stop for a minute to look at some tapestries that are bright and colorful and are embellished with images of our Lord holding small forest creatures. Elvis was still alive back in those days and the market hadn't blossomed yet.

I look over at Monroe and he looks just like all the hens do when a new rooster is turned loose in the pen. Then I see that Mama has popped a pair of Chiclets.

"Uh, Mama?" Monroe says. "How many of those have you had?"

"Six or seven," she shrugs. "You worried I might spoil my dinner?" And then she smiles at him.

We move on through the booths for about an hour until suddenly Mama gets this shocked look on her face, just like the time we had Roadmap over for supper one Sunday, and when she followed him outside to call him in for cake and coffee she caught him peeing off the front porch and talking to himself.

"Oh my," she says, and it's hard not to laugh even though I know she's embarrassed.

She looks around and we all know that there are no bathrooms at the Jockey Lot, and even if there were I wouldn't let my Mama use them.

"Come on, boys. We'd better go."

Then she takes off across the lot like those guys in the Olympics who have made walking a science and people don't want to tell them just how silly they look because they've worked so hard to look that way. Monroe and I have to jog just to keep up and Mama already has the car started and is gunning the engine when we get there.

"Move it or lose it," she says, and has her head cocked to one side to show she means it.

We no sooner pile in than she peels off. She sees a gas station open and cuts straight across eight lanes of traffic without even looking, causing all the cars coming and going to screech to a halt. She pulls into the station and parks all cattywampus and makes a beeline for the ladies room.

One of the guys who works there approaches her at a trot and says, "You can't park like—"

Only to get a stiff arm in the chest that has to surprise him coming from such a small and genteel person.

"Out of my way, Bud," she says. And that's that.

She never mentioned the incident but I think she finally figured out what happened.

That's okay, because I got even for her a few years later.

Monroe and I were both big pop drinkers. And since we rode the bus home together it became a contest just to see who could get to the refrigerator first. The old dirt road that led to our house was about a half mile long, and I usually won. Monroe was good for the first two hundred yards but then the bear would get him and he would start huffing and puffing and waggling his head from side to side, while I was just building up to a gallop.

I'd always catch him at about six hundred yards and he would always try to waylay me in some way. At first he'd just trip me, but later on when he got bigger and less patient and his hormones had kicked in with a vengeance, he'd just pick me up and chunk me across the fence into Old Man Argus's cow pasture.

That's when I first learned to deke and dodge, and I have

to admit that one of the greatest pleasures of my life was to be sitting on the stoop drinking my pop while Monroe trudged up the hill all red-faced and gassed-out. It was an extra special treat if the bottle I happened to be drinking was the last one in the carton.

One day Monroe learned a new trick. And that was to just thump me one in the stomach from the get-go and take off while I was bent double in pain and gasping for breath. I recovered and flew after him, and the closer I got the harder he struggled, until he was so put-out when I caught him that all I had to do was give him a little nudge toward the ditch, which was occupied at the time by briars so thick you could walk across them, and he tumbled headlong.

And there I sat, drinking my pop, when he stumbled toward the house looking like he'd had a run-in with a big switch and pulling thorns out of every conceivable part of his body. He didn't say a word as he went into the house, so I followed him, though out of arm's reach.

I had taken the first bottle out of a new six-pack and thought that once he saw the other five that would be the end of it. Instead, he opened all five bottles and took a long drink out of each one, making sure I saw him loll his tongue down into the gullet of every bottle. Then he put stoppers in the leftover bottles, took one with him, and gave me the smirk of victory.

The next day he was content to amble home in his own sweet time, knowing that I wouldn't touch the stuff. When he got there and saw me de-bottled he grinned and went in. He came out a minute later with a bottle, slurping and oohing and aahing like he'd just had an encounter with the Holy Spirit.

I moved out into the yard and said, "Good pop, Monroe?"

"Yeah boy." Then he gargled a mouthful before swallowing just to show me.

"Glad you like it," I said.

Then I zipped my pants where he could see me.

So everytime I come to the house Mama always asks me if I want a bottle of pop and I say 'no'. Then I ask her if she wants a Chiclet and she says 'no'. And we have good laugh.

"Are you listening to me?"

I realize that Charlotte has been saying something and I haven't got a clue what it is.

"You need to stop?" I ask innocently.

"No, you goof. Where were you?"

I smile a little. I can't help it. "Old days," I said.

"Were they good old days?"

"Yeah," I answer. "They were."

"I want to live out here some day," she says.

"In the boonies?"

"Away from town, anyway. Someplace where we can raise kids and feel good about it."

"We'll have to wait until Mrs. Bocook passes on," I say. "Unless you want to bring her along."

"You think so," Charlotte teases me, and then reaches over and pinches my belly.

I wouldn't have minded if I hadn't had to swerve to get out of the way of that vegetable truck.

We go into the trailer without knocking. That's something families do that will never change. I think that in ancient Egypt the kids of the Pharohs probably walked right in when they came for a little visit.

"Mama Nefertiti," I say.

She looks at me like I've lived in the city too long.

"Can I have a bottle of pop?"

"There's pop in the fridge."

"I got some Chiclets in my pocket."

But the simple truth is that I'm thirsty and go get a bottle.

"I'll pass on the Chiclets," she says.

I leave Charlotte to visit with her and go looking for Daddy. He's got his own little space, which I have come to believe is essential for every human being in this world. That if everybody had a little place to retire to whenever the spirit moved them we'd have a lot less problem getting along.

Daddy's is the barn. Well, it's more of an oversized shed than a barn. He's added on over the years and I can't look at it without thinking of Mr. Bocook. Not an animal's been allowed out there for as long as I can remember, not counting Monroe and the occasional wayward chicken. He keeps his tools out there, and even a little cot when he wants to sneak off for a little siesta.

He's working the lathe and I see that it's a duck decoy. I think. He's got one done and I hate to think it but it's the absolute worst duck decoy I've ever seen. It doesn't look like a duck at all. It looks like a coot on steroids. Either that or the result of some poor misbegotten crow who got amorous with a swan and somehow the Good Lord saw fit to let things work out.

"Jimmy," he says, looking up all proud. "What do you think?"

I wanted so bad to tell him that any duck who would bite on that one wouldn't be worth eating, but I hold my tongue.

"What kinda duck you reckon on luring?" I ask, which is a legitimate question.

He gets a disgusted look like he's wondering if I wasn't switched at birth.

"It ain't for huntin'. It's for show."

"Sir?"

"That there's high art, son. One of them he-she's in town said he'd give me a hundred dollars for every one I can turn out."

Don't get mad. There's just some things Daddy doesn't understand.

"You don't say," I say.

He nods and then turns back to the lathe, grinning to himself as he does.

"God, what foolishness people will spend their money on."

I smile and pat him on the back. He'll be seventy the next go 'round and I can't help but think about it. Maybe I should tell him about the glow-in-the-dark waterbed I found in Dumb Eddie's bedroom.

I start to help him like I used to when I was a chap. Which means that I try to do helpful things like move bits of wood out of his way but generally make a nuisance out of myself. He doesn't seem to mind as much as he used to.

When I go to get Charlotte she's got a little bag with her that looks like it was just dug up out of the yard. She doesn't say anything and I'm afraid to ask.

"And?"

"And what?"

"That bag."

"It sure took you long enough."

"Well, I thought maybe it was none of my business."

She reaches in and pulls out an old pink ribbon and an old blue ribbon, both of which look seriously used and give off an unkind odor. I recoil, I'm sorry to say.

"You don't like them?"

"What are they?"

"They're baby wishes, Jimmy."

"I wouldn't get a baby too close to them, honey. It might catch something."

"Don't be silly. That's just where they've had the works done to them."

Uh-oh. Mama and her hillbilly magic.

"What do you do with them?"

"They're for my pillow. Whichever you want, a boy or girl. You put it under your pillow until you conceive and that's what you'll get."

"Mama told you that."

"Yes. Who'd you think?"

"And you believed her."

"Not at first. But when she showed me how well they worked for her, I thought 'what's the harm'?"

"If they worked so well how come she's got two boys?"

"Oh, she said she never used the pink one. She wanted a

little girl, but by the time she was ready for you Monroe was already past two and she thought that having a little girl around might be kinda dangerous."

Which is why that night I dream about the time Monroe takes a bunch of sweat socks he's been saving from football practice all week and ties them up with a shoestring, then hangs them over my face while I'm sleeping. It's so bad my ears start ringing.

Then I realize that it's the alarm clock. And the first thing I notice is the smell. I start coughing and swinging my arms over my head.

"Get up quick, Charlotte. We've got a fire."

"Stop it," she says sleepily.

The smell is coming from her pillow. I rise in defeat and start to dress. Charlotte stirs and grins up at me and I sit down beside her and squeeze her a little, which is one of the purer joys of cohabitation.

"So which is it going to be?" I ask.

The smile she has is almost evil.

"Both," she says.

FOURTEEN

I call all the way through the M's for storage places and there is no Clarence, no Ducky, and the only Nash is a guy named Alfred, who I figure has problems of his own.

I decide to see if Ducky had a driver's license. Maybe I can run something through the DMV. While I'm at it I decide to do the same thing for Mr. Tannenbaum. Maybe I can get a better handle on him.

To do this, however, I have to get my boss's authorization, and I hate going to him even if the paperwork wasn't going to get drenched. But it's the price we pay for justice.

"I thought we agreed that you were going to leave this alone," he says, which naturally annoys me because 'we' didn't do diddly.

"Yes, sir, but I believe there is a connection between Mr. Nash (and I know Ducky's ashes do a spin in his vase when I call him 'Mr.') and Mr. Tannenbaum that might have resulted in his death."

"I don't know," he says, which in his case I'm sure that's the case at least half the time.

"Could be tax ramifications, too," I add.

He bites all the way to the bone.

"You think this man is a violator?"

"I think he's involved in laundering, sir."

What the heck. Mr. Big Boy hasn't spent the wee hours of the morning giving chase, now has he?

He studies the form, which is one of those in quadruplicate and NCR paper and I can see the PH changing colors on the corner where his fingers are. I'll probably have to have it dry cleaned even if he signs the damn thing.

"Can you make your case?"

"Not at the present time, sir, but I believe evidence was hidden by Mr. Nash (sorry again, Ducky) that would implicate Mr. Tannenbaum and unfortunately Mr. Nash was killed before revealing its location."

Not to mention that his wife is practicing Tae Kwon Do holds with a parole officer who's running the whole shooting match.

"I would prefer you give all the information to the police and let them handle it."

I knew that was coming. I sandbag it.

"Well, it's a little premature for that. What I'm trying to do is accumulate enough evidence to nail it down tight for them."

He starts to shake his head and I've got to move quick or else I'm going to get doused in the same way you get doused after giving your dog a bath.

"I believe I have the unofficial approval of the local F.B.I. office," I say, which is a real stretch, but so I'll owe him one.

He studies me for a second and then the form. He knows I'm wrong but he also knows my instincts are good. Or else that if I cause him grief he's going to lose the condom concession and maybe even a few brownie points with the Arch Revenooers in Washington. For all I know he's told them that he dreamed up the whole idea.

"Very well," he says finally, signing the form. The ink starts to spread halfway through his signature but he ignores it. "But if the shit starts to fly I'm finding an umbrella."

You mean like the Georgia Dome, Chubby? Okay, so I didn't really say it.

"I understand perfectly, sir," I say. "I'll take full responsibility."

I'm just about out when he stops me.

"Oh, by the way..." And believe me, I know it's bad news. "Washington is sending a man down to review your operation per our last discussion. A Mr. Lee. He'll be here first thing tomorrow, and I've assured them we'd provide our full cooperation."

Pig biscuits. That's all I need. Some wonk from Fantasyland poking around in my business when I've got so much of it to do. Sorry, Ducky, you lost out to a biff in a three-piece suit who's flying all the way down here just to see why I sell so many rubbers. Well, with a name like Lee he couldn't be all bad.

"Yes, sir," I say, before I really do say something I could regret, and also before I have to change my shirt.

Worried about drought? Famine? The depletion of the rain forests? The Greenhouse Effect?

Say no more.

For only nineteen-ninety-five you can rent...*The Human Cloud.* Just put him on a Nordic Track, keep him stocked with Gatorade, and I guarantee that within an hour there'll be big, fat, puffy clouds within a ten mile radius. Just call the Federal Building, Atlanta, Georgia. Ask for Jimmy.

My route gives me some desperately needed peace until I stop in at Miss Eva's Beauty Shoppe. She added the 'pe' to shop because she saw it that way on television.

Miss Eva is a very sweet lady I know from Rudy's. She could be fifty and she could be eighty. I can't tell and wouldn't dare ask. She's also got bright orange hair. I mean o-range. Her hair is so orange that Bozo the Clown would whimper. After we'd become friends I hinted around about it once and she told me she'd started doing it back in the sixties after getting her first color television and saw Lucille Ball, and didn't see any reason to stop just because Ms. Ball had gone on to meet her reward.

She wants to put one of my machines in her back room and I just about call 911.

"I know it might not bring you much," she says, "but I know you've got to stop in on old Snuff and he's just down the street."

"But Miss Eva," I explain. "I thought most of your customers were from church."

"That's my point," she says. "Some of them are widows

and Jimmy, they are scared to death."

"Well whatever happened to waiting until you were sure," I say.

I say this not as an indictment, but I've got to tell you that the thought of having to come in here and walk past all those sweet little old ladies with my satchel gives me heartburn.

"There ain't no such thing as 'sure' these days," she says.

Ain't it the truth. And so I put a machine in. It's as plain as they come and stocked strictly with skin-tone Regulars.

"I'm not worried about the money," I say in parting.

"You might be surprised," she says back, and then winks at me.

After that I wasn't sure what to do. So I decided to stake out Lee Sharpley's apartment. He's got to be doing business somewhere, checking in with Mr. Big and letting all the junior bad boys check in with him.

About five-twenty he pulls up in the Chevy and goes in. Maybe Slick and Dumb Eddie are waiting for him. Maybe all the guys from Sigma Nu are in there, too, and Lee is telling them that the best thing they could do is find Jimmy Nance and give themselves up.

Nope, I'm wrong. In twenty minutes he comes out and he's dressed like he's the guest speaker at the Jaycees Annual Dinner. He's also carrying a briefcase. If I didn't know better I'd think he was moonlighting as a C.P.A. This time he takes the Olds.

I follow him at a distance. I'm so good at it now that I put it on auto-pilot. We're headed for Buckhead. Mrs. Tannenbaum. Or it could be Mr. Tannenbaum this time.

Lee pulls into the driveway. There are no other cars around, but that doesn't seem to faze him. In fact he has a key. And he walks up to the door and lets himself in.

I see the lights go on inside. Nothing else happens. I wait around to see if there's going to be some kind of summit meeting or something, but nobody else shows. After about ten minutes he comes to the door dressed in a robe over sweatpants. He lets one of those little yapper dogs, the kind that God created the same day he created the Aardvark and Platypus, out for a tinkle.

Then I see the lady next door, who is at least sixty and built like Monroe, is wearing a string bikini and watering the lawn. She waves at me and smiles. I move out.

And find myself sitting outside Dumb Eddie's house. Well, not right outside his house. I'm not stupid. In fact I'm parked about four houses down and around the corner. He couldn't see me if he knew I was there. Don't bother to look when there's a dedicated R-Man on your trail.

I see two lights. One wavering in the living room, which I know to be that drive-in sized T.V., and one wavering in the back, which is know to be the hot tub.

I chuckle to myself, at first for the same reason I did before, and then because the wavering light surrounded by darkness makes me flash on when Monroe was baptized.

I don't honestly believe that Monroe was all that taken with the Spirit, but you couldn't play on the church basketball team unless you were a member, and you couldn't be considered a real member unless you had been dunked.

Monroe wasn't much good at basketball. But he was very good at wanton destruction. He had this one move we called the hang-yang-yang. Whoever the star was on the opposing team was the guy we always let Monroe guard. At some point early in the game the two of them would go up for a rebound amidst a cluster of other players, and the guy would always come down clutching his throat, while Monroe would miraculously appear thirty feet away with his head bowed in prayer.

That was the hang-yang-yang.

If Monroe was tired he became less subtle. He'd just heave an errant pass and whop the guy upside the head and render him unconscious, usually for the rest of the game. Sometimes for the rest of the season. And like all good Christians, Monroe would help him onto the stretcher amidst thundering applause.

We won the Championship the first two years and after the second trophy one of the other coaches demanded to see

Monroe's Certificate of Baptism, just to make sure that he was indeed a Holy Ghost Christian. So Monroe agreed to be baptized.

There was just one problem.

"I got to wear what?"

"This gown," Mama said.

"I ain't wearing no gown."

"It's not really a gown. It's a baptismal robe."

"What do I wear under it?"

That was adios, sayonara and bye-bye.

"Block that door, Jimmy!" Daddy said. "I'll head him off."

"Ooof."

"Jimmy? Jimmy, are you alright?"

"It wasn't no curveball, Daddy. I swear."

Mama saved the day. She came up with a compromise. He could wear his pajamas under the robe. Except that the only short pajamas he had was a Roy Rogers set with Roy, Trigger and the whole gang plastered all over them.

"Nobody'll see anything," Mama said. And that was that.

Roadmap wore hipwaders under his gown. We all thought that was cheating.

The church is silent and pitch-black except for the wavering light of the baptistry. Roadmap steps out into the water with his hands raised in supplication. Then Monroe moves into the trough and the water sloshes enough to make Roadmap lower his hands to grip the side. He loses his footing a little and starts to bob.

Mama has tears in her eyes and Daddy is clutching her hand. Fortunately it's the first Sunday of the month and he didn't have to rework his schedule.

The water settles finally and Roadmap takes Monroe under the chin. With both hands.

"James Monroe Nance. I baptize you in the name of the Father, the Son, and The Holy Ghost."

He manages to get him under but it's immediately obvious that he can't get him back up. Roadmap's got two handsful of hair and it's starting to look like high tide. Then Monroe starts to struggle and his gown takes on water like the Titanic until it billows up out of the water like a parachute. And everybody sees his Roy Rogers jammies.

It's still quiet and everything's okay until somebody whispers 'Yippie-tie-yie-yay' and the whole congregation breaks up. I know you probably think it was me, so same to you .

Monroe finally breaks the water gasping for breath and catches a mouthful of wet robe, and hears everybody laughing. He gets so mad that he grabs Roadmap by the head and holds him under and won't let him up, until all the Deacons have to make a rush for it and subdue him.

The choir got drenched, five of the Deacons needed minor medical attention, Monroe never got his Certificate and we never won another Championship.

Not long after that Roadmap retired for good and we joined another church.

It's after ten when Dumb Eddie and Slick come out and pile into the Gremlin. I wonder if Dumb Eddie ever got baptized. Maybe him and Slick take turns in the hot tub. Or at least see who can pee the biggest cloud.

There isn't another car in sight and I have to let them get a pretty good lead. I wish this was television. I could be right on their bumper and they'd never know it.

They hit I-75 and head north. Ninety minutes later we're still moving. I follow them all the way through Chattanooga, which I've heard is nice to drive through but terrible to live in, but they probably say the same thing about Atlanta.

Halfway between Chattanooga and Knoxville they exit off and pull into a place called Dee's Truck Stop. I pull in at the opposite side of the parking lot and watch.

Nobody moves. Well, the truckers coming in and out do, but Slick and Dumb Eddie don't. In about half an hour a big rig from Sears pulls up. The driver gets out and goes inside. You can see him through the window and he's headed for the john. I wonder who has the condom concession here.

That's when they make their move. Dumb Eddie just climbs into the rig and pulls off with Slick following in the Gremlin. I wish there was a soundtrack, because it's a little lackluster, I know.

I know what happens from here on out so I decide to stay put to see if the driver is in on it. He comes out of the john still fixing his fly, which is tacky even for Tennessee, and sits at the counter. No wonder Sears is having such a hard time.

It takes about forty-five minutes for the guy to eat. Then he goes back into the john. I could speculate, but why bother. Then he comes out. And if he's in on it then he should get an agent because he's wasting his time driving a truck.

He takes one look and starts waving his arms and jumping up and down like he just woke up from a bender up North and found an *I ♡NY* tattoo on his butte.

"Help! Help!" he hollers. "Somebody stole my truck!"

Then he dashes back inside and bypasses the john completely.

I see the crowd start to gather and look this way so I take my leave before the law arrives. I know I'm a witness but don't want to answer any questions just yet.

I've seen the cycle from start to finish and still don't have the slightest idea what to do. So I do the only logical thing I can think of. I go home.

It's the middle of the night when I get there and get into bed with Charlotte. The smell has changed, but not much for the better I'm sorry to say. Then I realize it's a combination of hand lotion and wish ribbons. It's pungent and loud and smells like show-and-tell at a podiatrist's convention.

She hears me sniffing and trying to clear my head and wakes up.

"Sorry I'm so late," I whisper.

She reaches over to pet me and I feel cold rubber on my skin and realize that she's wearing those heavy-duty gloves like Mrs. Monahan uses.

"What the—?" I respond, which I'm sure you'd do the

same if it was you.

"Sorry, Jimmy," she says, and pulls away.

"It's okay." And I pull her back.

I've adjusted to the light and see that she does have those gloves on only they're tied off at the wrists.

"You got lotion in those things?"

"Uh-huh. Full up."

"What happened?"

"One of the honchos at CNN keeled over at his desk today. We've got orders from the White House on down. I've got over two hundred just from Kuwait."

"Sorry you had a bad day," I commiserate.

"Bad your butt," she says in her half-asleep voice. "I pull this off and I'm set for the rest of the year. Which means I'm going to have to work late tomorrow."

"That's okay. I've got to entertain some bureaucrat from Washington."

"Man?" she asks.

"I presume."

"Okay."

"You still got both ribbons under your pillow?"

"I certainly do," she says, and there's a smile in her voice.

"Uh, you reckon they need anything to help them along?"

"I reckon they might. But I need to fix my hands."

"Leave them," I say, and pull her close.

"They might slosh," she whispers in my mouth.

"I hope so," I answer.

FIFTEEN

I don't have a rebellious bone in my body and whenever I get the urge to have a go at somebody I just take a nap. But today is different. So I don't wear a coat and tie, or even a tie for that matter, to work. If Mr. Lee really wants to know what's what he'll have to learn the same way I did, and that's driving around in the van and getting what you'd call hands-on experience.

I do decide to press my work clothes, though. No point in being disrespectful. My pants have a sharp crease. My shirt has had a good dose of Clorox 2. My brown shoes with the thick soles have a fresh coat of polish and I even give the strings a little dab and make sure they're poked in the right holes and in all the right directions.

I go straight into my boss's office and even before I get there I see the guy from the back and know that he's wearing a Brooks Brothers suit. Maybe I'll just introduce him to Lee Sharpley and they can compare socks.

I knock once and go in without being asked. And then I start grinning. I can't help it.

This Mr. Lee is actually Tommy Lee, who was an All-American guard at Georgetown until he got a knee all corrupted, and played about the same time I did.

"Tommy Lee," I say, extending my hand.

I don't think that he might think I'm just a big goofy yokel until it's too late. But then he starts grinning, too, and gets up to shake my hand.

"Jimmy Nance," he says. "When they told me who it was I didn't know if it was the same Jimmy Nance or not." And he gives my hand a good old-fashioned pump.

"You're probably thinking of my brother Monroe," I say, out of habit. "He played linebacker for the Saints."

"Yeah, I remember him, too. But you're the Jimmy Nance who played ball for Georgia State—"

"Georgia Southern."

"Yeah, yeah. You scored fifty points against Furman your junior year. Really blew them away."

"Forty-seven," I gently correct him, though I'm grinning like I just got the last cookie. And Tommy is still grinning, too, and still shaking my hand. "How'd you know about that?"

"My best buddy from high school played for Furman. I'm in rehab and he calls me like his mama just died and says this boy named Jimmy Nance tore him a new butt."

"Larry Wilkins?"

"One and the same."

Then we both crack up and start slapping each other on the back like long-lost kin and neither of us realize that my boss is just staring at us like we're two escapees from Fort Ho-Ho.

Tommy comes around first, which you'd expect from a real-life Washington Fed on somebody else's turf. He composes himself and reaches to shake my boss's hand.

"Thanks for all your help, sir," he says. "I'll take it from here."

And then he ushers me out of the office with his arm around my shoulder, which I think is extremely touching until I see that he's really drying his hand on my shirt.

"Hey," he says by way of apology. "These shirts cost sixty bucks a pop."

I take him to my little cubicle.

"So, what's the plan?" I ask.

"You look like you're dressed for work."

"Yeah. You bring any civvies with you?"

"Nothing with my name on the shirt," he grins.

"That's okay. Trainees don't get name tags."

Tommy's staying at the Omni International and we head that way. The streets of Greater Atlanta are crowded this time of day and I tell him it won't be so bad when we get to Lesser Atlanta, which is my turf.

"You think this is bad," he snorts. "You ought to try Washington."

We drive on and I still can't believe my luck. Tommy could've been All-Time All-Everything.

"Jeez, Tommy. How'd you come to be in such a situation?"

He gets this serious look on his face and I wonder if I've overstepped my bounds. Except that I know he wants to talk because he knows I'll understand, and in a minute he gets around to it.

"The knee was always bad," he says. "Ever since high school. People at Georgetown knew it. But I wanted to play and they wanted me to play. And they did me more good than harm."

He looks out the window and I know he ain't admiring the scenery, partly because the look in his eyes tells me he's going back, and partly because we're on the By-Pass and all you can see are the backsides of buildings.

"I wasn't really counting on going the four, anyway," he says. "I was just hoping for two good years and then enter the draft."

"The NBA," I say, and do it with a sense of reverence, and Tommy looks at me and we both understand.

"Yeah. The NBA. But after that game against Syracuse it was over. Still had my scholarship, though."

I think to myself that if they'd had Monroe, Tommy would have his own line of shoes now instead of riding in my van.

He looks at me. "So how about you?"

I grin. "Too short. Too slow. Hands too small."

Tommy grins back. "You missed your time, Jimmy Boy."

"How's that?"

"These days every team in the league would bend over backwards to have a decent white guy on their roster."

We laugh and I have to admit that I feel pretty good. And

it bothers me a little, too, not just because we've still got business to do, but because I thought I'd been feeling good all along and here I was feeling better.

"So why the Service?" I ask after a second. The Service is what we in the profession call it. It wouldn't be professional to ask 'How'd you come to be blood-sucking scum?'

"My old man's in the Service," he says. "A lifer. Got in his big five-seven last year. Him and Mama moved to Phoenix."

"You've obviously done well for yourself. Moving up the ladder and all."

Which was true. Tommy couldn't have been much more than a ten-year man and he was already two jumps up from my boss. Three from me.

"Well, I had three things going for me, Jimmy. One, my old man. Two, I'm ambitious."

"What's the third?"

Tommy looks at me like I've just spilled gravy on my pants and decided to walk around with the spot showing where it is.

"How many C.P.A.'s you know that are this dark?" he asks.

"Ah," I answer. "To tell you the truth, I really wasn't paying attention."

He reaches over and rubs my shoulder, like he'd just kicked my butt in a game of one-on-one and feels bad about it.

"I know," he says.

We get to the hotel and Tommy looks at me with a puzzled expression and I'm wondering if I've come to the wrong place.

"Jimmy," he says, "about your boss..."

I sigh out loud. I can't help it.

"Yeah?"

"Do you think he...knows?"

I sigh again. I can't help it.

"I honestly don't think he's got a clue."

Tommy shakes his head. "Too bad."

Tommy's idea of civvies is a maroon Nike jogging suit and white Adidas high-tops. He's got a white Polo shirt with thin maroon stripes and a gold chain around his neck. I'm giving him the once-over and he notices.

"Too much?"

"You look like a Republican hustler," I say.

"And..."

"You're supposed to be my boss."

"So wouldn't your boss naturally have more class than you?" he says, and backhands me one in the stomach the way guys like us have been doing ever since the first cavemen buddies did it by accident and liked it. "Besides, I thought I was a trainee."

"Okay. Lose the chain and the jacket."

He puts the chain in the pocket of the jacket and folds it very neatly on my toolbox. Except for the pants, which had zippers up the sides, he almost looked normal.

I work my route all morning and Tommy follows me around. Most folks are busy and there isn't time for introductions, except in Miss Eva's all the ladies get a gander at him and stop right in the middle of their gossip, which I wouldn't say if it wasn't so, and you could have heard a pin drop if not for the roar of the big hair dryers. Tommy is carrying my satchel and can already change out a machine, which speaks well of Georgetown, even though he's slow at it.

Miss Eva walks up and smiles and I can see Tommy trying hard not to stare at her hair.

"Is this young gentleman going to be working with you, Jimmy?" she asks, and her voice is so sweet you'd think she was auditioning to be the next Scarlett O'Hara.

"No, ma'am," I say. "Just a temporary helper."

Then we beg our leave and move toward the back.

"Close call," I whisper. "We could've been here all day."

"I can't believe you've got one of these machines in here with all those sweet little old ladies," he says.

"Hey, it was her idea."

We get back to the machine and I open it and just about get buried under the avalanche of quarters. Tommy starts laughing so hard that I'm glad the hairdryers are going—The machine is completely empty.

"I can't believe this," I moan.

Miss Eva walks back while Tommy is still trying to get control of himself.

"The first run might just be the novelty of it all," she says, all business. "But if this keeps up we'll have to talk about another machine. Maybe one with some colors this time."

"Yes, ma'am," I say, and I still can't look her in the eye.

She moves off and the only way I can get Tommy straightened out is to shove a couple of boxes at him.

"Here, trainee. Fill 'er up."

We're back on the road and I decide to take him the long way down Peachtree, which is not only a microcosm of Atlanta, but of the entire world. Everything in the whole unnatural universe can be found on some part of Peachtree Street, except for peach trees.

Tommy has settled back and I think he's starting to enjoy himself.

"So that's what you do," he says, and I know he doesn't mean anything disrespectful.

"That's the gist of it."

"I couldn't believe it when they showed me your numbers."

"Well, I've tried to establish a rapport with the people hereabouts."

"What about offenders?" he asks, and I know he's clicked into his working mode.

I look down the street and start pointing.

"There's a small-time casino operating above that laundromat. No cars allowed in the parking lot and they use a password system. I'm holding out until I know who all the principals are. See that garage? It's a chop-shop for stolen cars. Our guys are moving in next week. I've also got a lead on a new bookie."

Tommy nods in admiration.

"So what kind of network you got set up?"

"Nothing formal."

"Then how do you get your information?"

"People tell me."

"You mean you've got people on the payroll."

"No. I mean I sit around and chew the fat with people and they tell me things."

He shakes his head. "Unbelievable."

"Yeah, well you're in for a real treat now," I say.

"What's that?"

"I'm taking you to lunch at Rudy's."

We park and go in and I see Tommy looking around with a sad little smile like it all means something to him, but I don't pry. We go into the back to take care of business and I see Grady Tutwiler coming out of the men's room. He smiles at me and waves.

"New batch okay, Grady?" I ask.

"Would I be so happy if they weren't?"

Tommy looks at me. "Another satisfied customer?"

"Something like that."

We change out the machines, during which Tommy asks me to explain the principle behind The Missile, but I won't. So we go out and sit at the counter and wait for Rudy.

He's got a full house today and so he says his 'hellos' on the fly.

"Regular?" he asks.

"Two," I say. "With a side of hard cornbread and sweet tea."

He notices Tommy and nods, but then moves on.

"Oh by the way," I say. "You don't have hyperglycemia do you?"

"No," he says. "Why?"

I just shake my head.

I watch as he takes his first sip of tea and seeing it ranks right up there with the first time Charlotte and I... well, never mind.

"Whoo-ha," he says, and I know his roots are showing.

"Ain't it the truth," I answer.

"He ought to bottle that stuff."

"The people at Coke would pay him a billion dollars not to."

He takes another big gulp and then makes a satisfied sound that comes from deep down. Rudy brings our lunch and pulls up a stool to watch and make sure everything's hunky-dory, but also to get the low-down on Tommy.

Tommy takes his first bite and smiles. Rudy smiles back and a friendship is born. Then something amazing happens.

"Red bean casserole with onion and brown sugar," Tommy says.

"You don't mean it," Rudy answers.

"God, it's been years."

Rudy looks at him with genuine affection. The same way he always looks at me.

"Boy, you've been away too long."

Then they both look at me to let me know I've shirked my duties.

"Rudy, this is Tommy Lee. He's one of the bosses where I work. Tommy, this is Rudy, the proprietor of this establishment."

They shake and exchange greetings. We dig in and Rudy gets up to leave. Then I see him give me a quick glance out of the corner of his eye and I know I'm in trouble.

"Mr. Lee," he begins.

"Tommy."

"Tommy, then. I don't want to interrupt your lunch, or to have you think I was politickin' or anything like that, but I feel it's only right to tell you that Jimmy here is just about the best rubber man in the whole Southeast."

Somebody chokes on tea and coughs. I think it's me.

"Rudy," I wheeze.

"He's thorough. He's efficient. He's conscientious. He don't leave no mess or do anything that would offend anybody."

"Rudy," and it sounds like Beverly Sills doing The Godfather.

"And bless his heart, if there is ever any kind of conflict over quality or maybe some money the machine ate Jimmy don't even question. He just does what's right."

"Rudy," and it sounds like Juliet's death scene.

Without missing a beat Rudy draws a glass of water and shoves it in front of me.

"Shush, Jimmy. You need a little braggin' on. So let me tell you the true facts, Tommy, with all respect and professional courtesy. If you ever replace this boy here with anybody else you're going to lose a whole lot of business."

Then he nods and that's that.

I try to sip the water. My throat feels like I ate about ten sheets of number 6 sandpaper. I also know that I've turned the color of a librarian the first day of summer vacation, but Tommy just takes it all in, between mouthfuls of course, and then speaks in a voice so serious you'd think he was an undertaker.

"Don't trouble yourself, Rudy. Jimmy here ain't going nowhere."

Rudy finally heads off, and then almost as an afterthought, turns to me.

"Oh by the way. Flora Watkins is at it again."

This does surprise me. "I thought she was in jail."

"Well she's out now. And she's set up shop above old Henry Auger's ice cream place. You might want to talk to him about some machines before there's a tragedy."

"Thanks," I say.

He nods again and then to Tommy as he moves away.

"Nice to meet you," Tommy says.

"You, too," Rudy replies. "And sorry about your knee."

We're back on the road and feeling like a couple of Romans. Rudy has given us what was left in the casserole pan, which is about four servings, and I invite Tommy to finish it off at my house for supper. He accepts.

"I see what you mean," he says after a time.

"About what?"

"About everything. He knew who I was without saying anything and he gave you Flora Watkins, who I presume is running girls."

"I had her popped last year."

"And he cares about you. All of them do."

"Yeah."

"And you hate it because you're undercover."

"Yeah. I do."

"He wouldn't care," Tommy says.

"I like to think that way, too. But it bothers me. I can't get around it."

Then he gets that same look I saw when we first went into the place.

"My grandfather had a place like that in Baltimore," he says. "He made stuff like this casserole. He could take any two cans off the shelf and make a meal out of it and once you had it, you'd never forget it. I would've lived in that place if my old man hadn't raised Hell all the time."

"He didn't like you hanging out in there?"

Tommy shook his head. "He was ashamed."

"Why?"

"He didn't want his son spending his whole life in colored town."

I've got nothing to say to that. "What happened to the place?"

"It died when he died."

Then he sighs and gets himself back. He's been himself for so long now that there isn't the time or the inclination to be anybody else.

"I do know one thing, though."

"What's that?"

"What you do here can't be duplicated, at least not by most agents. The people in Washington wouldn't understand in a million years and I can't explain it to them. I can see my report now...'RE Investigator James Nance, Atlanta, Georgia. His cover operation is so successful because he visits a lot. And his investigations are so successful for the same reasons. The people in the community just wait for him to come along so that they can tell him everything that's going on.' "

"Yeah, I guess it would sound sort of strange. I tried to tell my boss that but..."

"But he's a bureaucrat trained the DC way and wouldn't get it if it sat in his lap and called him Sweetie."

I nod. Then a chill runs up my back. I can't help it.

"Yeah, that was kind of gruesome. Sorry."

"That's okay. So, you want to go back to the hotel?"

He smiles. "I thought we had more machines to change out."

I smile back. "We do."

"Then let's hit it."

SIXTEEN

We pull up in front of Arnold Carvey's house and Tommy looks at me like the wing-nut just flew off my bolt.

"You don't have machines in here," he says.

"I want you to meet somebody."

Arnold comes out with the basketball under his arm and scowls at me.

"Guy you told me about won't do business with me."

I shrug. "Maybe you should concentrate on other areas.

"God," he snorts. "Grownups suck."

"I brought somebody by to see you," I say, as my way of making up for my sub-species. "Arnold, this is Tommy Lee. Tommy, this is Arnold Carvey."

Tommy shakes his hand but Arnold is suspicious.

"He another G-Man?"

"Yeah," I say. "He was also an All-American at Georgetown."

Arnold doesn't bite. "So how come I never heard of him?"

Arnold has an old rusty rim nailed to the side of the house. He gets big enough to dunk and I think that maybe the wall won't survive it.

"Because you were about two years old during my golden days," Tommy says.

And he scoops the ball away so quick that Arnold doesn't even react until the ball is flying. It's twenty-five feet but it sails through the hoop without touching metal.

Arnold grins and runs down the ball. He gives Tommy a bounce pass and Tommy does a quick dribble between his legs and hits a running hook from twenty.

He is so fluid that I can't stand to watch and can't stand to look away. He is every ballplayer's dream and every ballplayer's nightmare. He has something so perfect and pure that those of us who don't and have to sweat and strain every inch of the way want to strangle him, but our love for the game stirs something stronger within us that wants to make him God.

Tommy gives Arnold a perfect pass on the run and Arnold moves in for the layup. He is still a kid, still elbows and knees and looks like a new colt. But the power is there if he wants it. He can play ball now, but in a few years he'll be a ballplayer.

He moves out and Tommy snags the rebound and hits him chest-high. Arnold fakes left and swings to the right, that first taste of perfect motion right on the tip of the tongue that sticks out a little as he rises for the shot. It bounces around a little but falls through.

I move out of the way. This has nothing to do with me. I just lean against the van with my arms folded and watch the glory of potential.

They fall into a pattern without speaking a word. Tommy does something and Arnold imitates him. When he can't execute Tommy does it again, exaggerating a little to show him what he did wrong. Arnold gets better each time. And the only sounds are feet shuffling on the dusty ground, the ball against the worn-out wood and metal, and the traffic on the street behind me.

Twenty minutes pass and they're still at it. The ball bounces free and Tommy can't resist going in for a backward jam. The ball flies through and hits the ground before he does and jumps straight back into the air. Tommy hits the ground hard and his bad knee reminds him that now he's just a mere mortal approaching middle-age. He winces a little and bows out, but the smile on his face stretches from coast to-coast.

Arnold follows after him wearing a look of awe and concern.

"That why you didn't turn pro?" he asks.

Tommy nods. "More or less."

Arnold pauses. "Do I have the stuff?"

Tommy smiles. "Yeah, kid. You've got the stuff. You playing ball anywhere?"

"Pick-up games around the neighborhood. Can't go out for junior high ball until next year and three years until high school."

Tommy takes the ball and spins it from his index finger to his pinky, switching hands with the ball still whirling.

"Go to the Y. The Boy's Club. Jimmy here'll help you."

Yeah, I thought to myself. I'll get Monroe to teach you the hang-yang-yang.

Then I see that he's watching me expectantly.

"Yeah, I'll ask around."

"Thanks," he said. And I could tell by the way he said it that he wasn't used to it, maybe because he'd never had much occasion before.

We're standing near the van and getting ready to leave when Tommy takes one dribble and launches the ball. He's got to be forty feet away but the ball goes through without so much as a whistle.

"You take care of yourself now," he says to Arnold.

Arnold watches the shot and then looks at Tommy. "I will."

We leave and I can see Tommy trying to keep his leg straight and grunting low every time it moves. Some wounds never really heal.

"You need an ice pack?"

"Yeah. Where we headed?"

"Home. Unless you need to run by the hotel first."

He shakes his head. "I do this about once a week. I'll be okay until we get to your house. Usually it happens doing something useless, like getting out of the car wrong. Don't seem to hurt as bad this way."

"You missed your calling," I said.

"I wouldn't have passed the physical."

"No, I'm talking about coaching."

He shakes his head and I can see the poison well up. And I understood. It was all or nothing with him. Then he grins a little by way of apology.

"This kid, Arnold. How'd you meet him?"

I think about Ducky and my heart does a dip. I don't know what else to do so I tell him. I tell him the whole thing. I tell him about Ducky and how I found him dead and how I know that some people are running a major stolen goods operation out of a warehouse in Tucker and how it's all tied in somehow, but exactly how, I don't know. I don't know what I expected, either. I didn't feel much better after the telling.

"You're going to have to move pretty quick, or it's going to get away from you," he says, now in his work mode again.

"I know," I answer.

"Jimmy."

His voice sounds kind of harsh at first, but when I look I realize that he just wanted to get my attention to show that he empathizes.

"Yeah?"

"You ain't never going to know who killed that boy."

I heave a long sigh through my nose. If Charlotte was here she'd be irked at me.

"Maybe you're right."

"Great Gog a Mogey," he says.

We're pulling into the driveway and Tommy gets a gander at my garage.

"Need any Christmas ornaments?" I ask.

Then I tell him about Mr. and Mrs. Bocook. He loses it so bad that I have to help him up the steps, which I was planning to do anyway because of the knee, but which now has become a necessity.

We get into the house and I point to all the rooms, giving him the one-finger tour while he eases onto the couch. I bring him an ice pack and I've got to admit that when he pulls up his pants leg it's the ugliest thing I've ever seen next to the back of Monroe's head.

I start to fix supper. I heat Rudy's leftover casserole in the microwave. I've got some store-bought cole slaw and cut up a couple of yellow apples. I pour the tea and we move to the table.

"Sorry I'm not going to get to meet Charlotte," he says.

"Me, too."

"Special, is she?"

I smile. I can't help it. "More than special. She's unique."

"And you'd die without her."

"Yeah. I would."

Then he pulls out his wallet and shows me a picture of a woman and two girls.

"This is Laura, my wife. The oldest girl, Beverly, is seven. Shawna is four."

I look. Laura is a stunner and the older girl looks just like her. The baby looks just like Tommy, but maybe she'll outgrow it.

"Got any ballplayers in the bunch?"

Tommy grins and shakes his head. "They don't even know about that stuff. Well, Laura does. She's been with me since high school. I'd never have made it without her. But she stuck. Gives me a sense of continuity, you know?"

I nod. I really didn't know. My life has come in stages and when one stage ended the people who were a part of it seemed to fall by the wayside somehow.

We eat and joke and tell war stories about the old days with an occasional story about the Service. Tommy tells me about his boss, who's tall and skinny and looks like Eb on Green Acres.

We're like two long-lost buddies who get together after so many years to reminisce even though we just met this morning. It's silly, I guess, but I think we both realize that there is an important part of our lives that came and went but left its mark, and neither of us has the chance to talk about it much even though we both still feel it.

After supper I give him the grand tour. There isn't much

to see so it doesn't take long. I save the bedroom for last and when we get there I see Tommy's nostrils flare, which is probably involuntary on account of they don't really want to deal with it.

"You got critters?" he asks.

"Well, it's kind of hard to explain. See, Charlotte got these ribbons from my mother she claims are baby wishes, if you can believe that."

"Say no more," Tommy says, holding up a hand to stop me. "I've had to deal with some voodoo myself."

"Yeah?"

"How do you think I got two daughters?"

We retire to the veranda, which means we go outside and sit on the top step. It's cool and clear and all the stars are there to give us a howdy-do. Tommy sips his tea and twirls his ice around, and I think he's got a taste for something stronger but I can't accomodate him and he doesn't ask.

"How's the knee?"

"Like somebody drilled a hole, stuck in a sixteen penny nail. And is playing the cymbal part in the 1812 Overture on it with a ballpeen hammer."

"Graphic," I say. "You should be a writer."

"How about lawyer?"

"That's all we need. More lawyers."

Then he grins mischievously. "Well that's what I'm going to be in about six months."

"No kidding?"

"The Service is putting me through law school. I've got one term to go. Then I'll owe my soul to the company sto', but at least I'll get to go one-on-one with the bad guys in court."

"That's great, Tommy."

"What about 'that's all we need. More lawyers'?"

"Yeah, but you could really do some good."

"Well, let's hope so. It also means that my job will be

open. Interested?"

I didn't know what to say. "I don't know what to say." See, I told you.

"Would you be interested?"

"There's got to be a line butt-deep for that job."

"Yeah, but I can recommend anybody I want. Law of the jungle."

"But why me? I'm just a low-ender."

"This job is analyzing the data of a couple hundred agents doing what you do every day. You know how it works. You could be a tremendous asset."

"How about promoting my boss and giving me his job?"

"Wouldn't work," he says. "We'd have to keep him in some kind of spacesuit."

"Well, that's true."

"I know it's a lot to think about. But would you give it some consideration?"

"Sure. But I've got to be honest, I'd never get Charlotte out of Atlanta."

Which is one of the biggest whoppers I've ever told, and done at the expense of my one and only love. So bury me in dirt up to my chin and come at me with a weed whacker. The truth is, I didn't want to move.

"I know it would be a change, but at least think about it, okay?"

"Okay."

I have to admit, I was flattered. Upward mobility and all that. But they'd probably put some ying-yang on my route and he'd ball it up.

After a second Tommy looks at me again.

"Jimmy?"

"Huh?"

"You really think I'd be a good coach?"

"Yeah, Tommy. I do."

"Maybe I'll look into it when I get back."

"Well if it doesn't work out you've always got a job with

me. I've been thinking about expanding."

"Jimmy Nance. The Condom Czar of the South."

"And you could get in on it."

"Would I get my own van?"

"Eventually."

"With 'Here Comes Tommy Lee' painted on the side?"

"If that's what you wanted."

"Would I get to learn what The Missile is?"

I laughed. "Naw. You've got to be at least a third degree rubber man for that."

"What's first degree?"

"The easy stuff. Rudy and Miss Eva."

"Does she know her hair is that orange?"

"I got no idea."

"So what's second degree?"

"You've got to be able to change out a machine in Snuff Waldrep's without getting sick."

"I could do that."

"Yeah, well you had it easy. There weren't no trade-ins today."

"I was wondering why you had those gloves in your box."

"So now you know."

"What's third degree?"

"The third degree comes in three parts."

"Naturally."

"The first is that you've got to eat lunch with my brother, Monroe. And sit right across from him."

"That bad?"

"Well, he did play in the NFL for seven years."

"Okay. If I do that, what?"

"You've got to be able to catch a machine-load of quarters in your pocket without dropping any.

"Easy," he says. "What's part three?"

"You've got to spend twenty minutes in my boss's office—"

"I did that—"

"In July when the air conditioning's out."

Tommy shudders. "No way. Guess I'm stuck with being a government lawyer."

"Well, we've all got to have dreams."

We settle back and fall quiet and sip our tea for awhile. Tommy seems to take it all in. And when he speaks again it's very soft, as if he wants to make sure he doesn't violate the Life enclosing us with the timbre of his voice.

"You've got a special life, Jimmy. Full of love and friends and contentment. I hope it never changes for you."

I don't know how to answer because I know he's right. Charlotte'll be home in a little while and the house will brighten as if it has been waiting for her, too. I'll go to work tomorrow and share a hundred smiles. And there will always be Tuesdays to look forward to.

"I'm sure you have that, too," I say finally.

"Some," he says. "But mostly what I've got is politics."

Then he scrunches down a step so that he can look straight up into the sky, as if it was about to change and wouldn't look like this for awhile.

"So what do you think, Jimmy?"

I watch him for a moment. I think he's just as lost as he is found, and has to spend most of his time walking that curb.

"I think you had the stuff, Tommy," I say.

He drinks the rest of his tea in one gulp, and the ice rattles as a reminder that you can't keep noise from the calm any more than you can keep clouds from the stars. And his voice is so small that if I wasn't looking I'd have thought it was a child.

"Yeah. Maybe I did."

SEVENTEEN

I take Tommy to the airport the next morning. I don't have to, but I want to give him one last ride in the van as sort of a big send-off. All we talk about is the Service and I know he's already switched into his Washington mode. I don't want to cast a damper on anything, but as I wave good-bye I know he'll have a couple of drinks on the plane and still be wound tighter than a golf ball when he lands.

I also know that I won't take the job even if it's offered. Still, I can't help thinking about the promise of things, and how it is sometimes taken away from us, but how promise always exists even if in different shapes and forms and people, and is ready for us when we are ready for it.

Five years from now Tommy Lee will probably be the best litigator in the Service. Arnold Carvey will be a high school star with every college scout in the country drooling over him. Charlotte and I will have a couple of kids and Miss Eva will have eight machines in her shoppe.

Ducky will still be dead.

I work the rest of the alphabet and still no warehouse is rented in the name of Clarence, aka 'Ducky', Nash. The very last place in the phone book is Z & Z storage, and is owned by a guy named Zumsari, and one of his kin I would guess.

I can tell when I talk to him that not only is he foreign, but fairly newly arrived at that.

"I'm looking for a warehouse rented in the name of Clarence or Ducky Nash," I say.

"Dookey?" he says.

"Ducky."

"Quack-quack Dookey?"

"Yeah, that's his name."

"No dooks. Storage."

"I know that. Ducky is his nickname."

"No dooks. Storage."

If I was a vindictive person I'd have him audited. Welcome to America.

I know it's almost over. There's nothing else I can do. The only thing left is to make sure the goods from the last Sears truck are where I think they are, because if they aren't when the cops roll in I'm going to have a lot of explaining to do. So I need to get a whiff of this loft in City's warehouse.

I don't even have to wait until the middle of the night for this one. By six-thirty the place looks like Sunday night at a Catholic church, and I'm parked down the street and ready to make my move.

I walk across the parking lot keeping the rows of vehicles between me and the main entrance, where I presume the guard is stationed. I get there and sure enough the place is locked up tighter than a nun's boudoir. The only light I see from inside is coming from a window adjacent to the main doorway.

I stand there for maybe twenty minutes until he comes out. I don't want to sound unkind but the guy looks just like Mr. Potato Head except that on top of the potato is another head, this one wearing one of those Smokey Bear hats. I also wonder how they make britches that would hold that shape.

He's got a flashlight even though it's broad daylight and I can see Ducky up in heaven grabbing Allan Pinkerton by the sleeve and pulling him over to see this guy, and then elbowing him in the ribs. At least he heads around toward the back first and that gives me all I need.

Naturally the door is locked. It's also one of those heavy-duty double locks and I couldn't pick it with a hatchet. The window is a solid piece of glass that doesn't open, and even if it did is about eight feet off the ground. All the bay doors are closed but I jump up on the edge of the dock. There's only a six-inch ledge and it's precarious enough just standing there, not to mention that when I reach down to pull up on the door it's locked, too, and I fall off onto the asphalt and tear my pants. And Allan Pinkerton elbows Ducky in the ribs.

I don't know what else to do but just sit there on the step until Spud comes back. Maybe I can sweet-talk him.

When he does he's heading up the fenceline and doesn't even see me.

"Hey," I holler at him.

He jumps but doesn't want to let on, so I let him off the hook and give him my truest smile.

"I left my lunch box inside," I say.

What the Hell, he works nights and probably doesn't know me from any of the other criminals.

He nods and comes right to the door. He unlocks it and lets me in.

"Make sure it closes good behind you," he says, "or it won't lock."

"Thanks," I say, and I'm in.

All the offices are cubbyholed to the right so I make a beeline for the back. To the left are the locker rooms and straight through is the warehouse proper.

I yell out 'hello!' just to make sure I'm alone, and when nobody answers I move in.

The part Mr. Delray told me about isn't hard to find. It's all the way back in the far left corner. Sure enough there's a big metal gate to the stairway and it's locked solid. I move under the floor from one end to the other. I get all the way to the far end before I see a little gap in the plywood flooring.

I've got no way to get up there and I've got a vertical leap of about a foot-and-a-half. So I commandeer a fork lift. Hey, I'm a federal officer duly executing his chosen profession, even if I don't have a warrant and am in fact trespassing. Once I'm out of here, do what you want.

I hike the forks up past the top of the cab and climb up. I'm still not quite high enough to reach and it's frustrating. I think that maybe I should just go get Spud to help me but he might catch on. So I clamber down and find a piece of rope.

I tie it to the control lever and get back up on the forks. I should hire myself out to one of those companies that makes industrial movies about trying to cut down on lost-time accidents.

"*See this man. Don't do this!*"

I pull on the rope and it works like a charm. I'm on my way up and Ducky slaps Allan on the back and gives him a friendly thumb to the nose.

Except a rope is what you'd call a flexible thing as opposed to an inflexible thing, which means I've got no way of reversing the process. So the forks keep moving toward the floor of the loft and I'm about four feet away from getting squished. And Allan snorts at Ducky and calls over his buddies to watch.

I can see it now. They'll peel me off the bottom of that grating looking like a Belgian Waffle. Tom Brokaw will be wearing his most sincere expression of woe and cut to Irving R. Levine.

Mr. Potato Head will say I overpowered him with tear gas.

Mr. Tannenbaum will call it a senseless tragedy that comes from an undisciplined government, and will be elected to Congress with Lee Sharpley as his chief aide.

My boss will offer *no comment* then will mistake the news van for a donut truck and have to be restrained, and finally put down by an elephant dart.

Charlotte will be crying buckets and ask how I came to be in such a predicament.

Mrs. Bocook will step right up to the camera and say,

"Well, he always was a little odd."

And then it stops. On its own. Apparently it ran out of track about a foot-and-a-half from the floor. I'm lying flat on my back by this time, but I'm alive. And once I get my breath back, and my heart stops sounding like the drum solo in *In A Gadda Da Vida*, I'll be okay.

I wish I had Spud's flashlight because it's darker than my

garage up there, and just as mysterious. I manage to stick my fingers through the grating and touch a carton that straddles the gap in the plywood. It's heavy, but I can rock it enough to see the word 'Sears' on the side with 'VHS' as part of the description. I crane my neck and am able to see that there are boxes stacked to the ceiling. I deduce that there are a lot more up there or else why would these need to be stacked to the ceiling?

I figure Ducky and Allan are about even now, and it shifts back to Ducky's favor when I'm able to climb down the forklift without injury, and only tear my other pants leg once, even if I do have a flashback and hear *Silent Night* ringing in my ears.

I put the forklift back the way I found it and make it outside before the guard gets back from his rounds. I reach behind me to make sure the door is locked, just like I promised.

Then I scoot.

I get home and Charlotte has a pretty dress on and is the perfect picture of loveliness.

"We going out?" I ask. Which I suppose I've got as much right to ask as anybody.

"What happened to your pants?"

"It's a long story. So are we?"

"Mrs. Bocook invited us to supper at her house."

I scowl and Charlotte scowls back at me.

"Now be nice, Jimmy. That old lady just worships you and is only trying to treat us like family."

"The Addams Family," I mutter. "And that ain't my concern."

"What's your concern?" And I can tell she's getting a little impatient with me.

"How are we going to find the dining room? And if we do, how are we going to get out again?"

She thumps me on the arm and I know I've got no more say in the matter. But since it's important to Charlotte I shower and dress and put on a nice tie.

She takes my arm as we walk next door. Mrs. Bocook

answers and looks at both of us as if we'd just got off the wrong bus.

"Who died?" she asks.

"Nobody, Mrs. Bocook. Charlotte said we're invited for supper."

"Oh. So you are. If I'd known you were going to take it so serious I wouldn't have bothered."

And then she just leaves us standing in the doorway, which is her way of telling us to follow her, which is no small task. I roll my eyes and Charlotte pinches me and mouths 'be nice', which is no small task, either.

I try holding her hand and that's an even greater challenge. My shoulder scrapes an eight-foot stack of National Geographics and we nearly buy it right there amongst the critters of New Guinea. We try to work our way through and I start to feel like the guy in King Kong who has to cut his way through the jungle for the sake of his honey only to be punched out by a big ape.

After a minute Charlotte decides to drop in behind me and puts her hands on my waist as if we're doing the conga. I should have worn a pith helmet. Johnny Weismuller, where are you when we need you the most?

After a close encounter with a mountain of old hardcover books which smell a lot like Charlotte's wish ribbons, and taking *Billy Budd* which I was supposed to read once but faked it with the Cliff Notes and still pulled a B-, on the head, we find a clearing. It's the dining room.

It's been pared down to an area just big enough for the table and chairs, surrounded by stacks of old China and the Bocook's household records from 1928-1963, but we can at least sit down.

The table is nice, though, and Mrs. Bocook has made pot roast, potatoes and carrots, honey-baked rolls and some red-looking stuff in a little bowl that sort of reminds me of JuJubes in their most natural state. Maybe she found them on the window sill somewhere after twenty years or so and thinks they're still good.

"That's cranberry relish," Mrs. Bocook says, giving me a look like I'm the dumbest creature on earth.

I take a sip of my tea and just about gag. It's loaded with artificial sweeteners, which is one of the most assinine concepts of the modern age. The companies that make it spend billions on advertising to make us believe how good it tastes when we all know you could suck on your socks and never know the difference.

They should let me do the commercials.

"We're here with Edith Spivey of Four Corners, Georgia, for a blind taste test. First we make sure the blindfold is in place."

"Hey, you got my wart bent double there, Junior."

"Sorry. Now take a sip from Glass A."

"Tastes like my back yard."

"Okay, now suck on these for a minute."

"I can't taste no difference."

If you don't want sugar in it, then why don't you just leave it alone.

"Jim, you're the man here," Mrs. Bocook says, and does it like she's questioning the very statement as she speaks.

Then she bows her head like Mother Theresa. "Please ask the blessing."

I almost say the prayer Monroe used to say before Sunday dinner.

Father, Son, Holy Spirit. I'll kick your butt if you get near it.

But I don't.

"Bless us O Lord and these Thy gifts which we humbly receive from Thy bounty, Amen."

We start digging in and I'm a little surprised to discover that it's a mouthful. Except that I'm already suspicious. Mrs. Bocook has brought me a drink or two whenever I was out in the yard doing work for her. Occasionally she would make me a baloney sandwich. But never a spread like this. I also remember the last time we talked and wonder if whatever she has to say is going to ruin my supper.

And I don't have to wonder long.

"I think it's time you two contemplate the future," she says.

"Ma'am?" And I almost get a piece of carrot hung.

"Seems that some time back I promised you that building over there when I died."

"Well, that's a long way off, I'm sure."

"Shush it," she says. "Don't interrupt your elders. Anyway, the simple fact is that I thought I'd be dead by now. Don't ask me why I ain't. Weren't my decision."

I'm thinking she's going to renege on the deal and that's okay because all-in-all she's been very good to us.

"You're more important to us than that," Charlotte says.

Mrs. Bocook looks at her and smiles all gooey, which is in itself a frightening thing.

"The thing is," she goes on, "I want you to have some security. I want you to have your own place where you can put down roots and be happy. So one day next week I'm going to take old Leadbutt here down to that useless lawyer of mine in town and deed you over the building and the three acres around it."

I'm still trying to get over Leadbutt when what she's saying hits me. Fair market value is over eighty thousand dollars. I'm ashamed to admit it, but my first thought is how I can pull it off without paying taxes on it. If I wasn't so hungry I'd cry.

"Including that old oak tree out back?" Charlotte asks, and her excitement is tangible.

"Yes, dear. And if we can get this boy's equipment workin' your children will have a swing out there someday."

Charlotte looks at me with tears in her eyes. I've got a mouthful of potato so all I can manage is to blink at her. She doesn't seem to mind.

Then she gets up and hugs Mrs. Bocook so hard that I worry she might snap her backbone. And one of the most curious things I've ever encountered happens. I hear a sniff. And it ain't me and it ain't Charlotte.

"Shush now," Mrs. Bocook says, and pats Charlotte on the arm and shoos her away.

Then she turns to me and I don't know if I'm ready for such sentiment.

"Clear the table, Leadbutt," she says.

Then she gets up and takes Charlotte with her.

I clear the table and put the leftovers in the fridge. I'm astonished to find the kitchen completely uncluttered. Well, we've all got our little hangups. I rinse the dishes and put them in the sink to soak. I'm just about done when I hear someone in the doorway.

I turn around and it's Mrs. Bocook standing there in a very sheer, shorty nightgown. I recoil, I'm sorry to say.

"Ah, don't be such a weenie, Jim," she says. "I know you're spoken for. Lock up when you leave. I'm going to bed."

As I walk across the yard I see Charlotte standing near the oak tree out back. It's older than America and at least six feet across, with great and mighty arms. It's dark, but there's a security light farther down that makes her hair look as if it's glowing.

I get there and she hugs me and we don't say anything for a long time.

"I know you've been feeling a lot lately," she whispers. "About Ducky and your family, and having Tommy Lee around made you miss having buddies some of the time."

I stroke her hair. "You should go to work for Madame Ruth."

"You need those feelings so that you'll know what's really important to you. So that you won't look back some day with regret."

I push her away from me, but very gently and only so that I can look at her.

"I know what I want and what I don't want."

She takes my hand and leads me to a spot of ground that's flat and overlooks a little valley that leads to the woods, where wildflowers turn it into a meadow every spring.

"What don't you want?" she asks.

"I don't want to fight my way up the company ladder. I don't want to leave Atlanta. I don't want to sit around all day long and talk about the good old days the way Monroe does, and I don't want to pretend that I could've been a star and got cheated, because that's not the way it was."

"What do you want?"

"I want you. I want us. I want what we've got right now to keep getting better."

She stands away from me and moves into the meadow.

"The front porch would be right here so that we could sit out at night and watch the lightning bugs as they come out of the woods."

I move closer to her. "Yeah?"

"And it would have two stories and high ceilings and built to look old even though it wouldn't be."

I grin. "How many bedrooms?"

"Three," she says, "with a couple of rooms that could be made into bedrooms later on should the need arise."

"Sounds like you've got it all figured out."

"How much would something like that cost?"

I cringe a little but smile through it.

"I don't know, honey. How much have we got in our rainy day fund?"

"About a hundred and eighty dollars."

"Well, we'll just have to keep working on it."

"I'm serious, Jimmy."

I sigh. I can't help it. "I don't know exactly."

"Guess."

"Considering we'd have to furnish it, and depending on how much grading costs , and what we actually decide to build and how much of the interior we could do ourselves—"

"How much, Jimmy?"

I look at her and my heart breaks into a jillion pieces. This is one of those times when I wish I could say anything but the truth.

"Over a hundred thousand dollars, Charlotte. There's no way around it."

She nods like it doesn't even phase her. "I've got something to show you," she says, and hands me a little book.

I take it and see that it's a passbook from one of the local Savings & Loans, which if I'd known she'd put money in there I'd have told her to put it in a coffee can and bury it in the yard.

I twist toward the light and can barely make out the numbers. She's been saving regularly week by week. She's got a little over seven thousand dollars and it makes me want to cry.

"You've saved seven thousand dollars," I say. "That's really great, sweetheart."

"Some accountant you are," she says.

So I look again. And see that it's SEVENTY thousand dollars.

"Jesus Henry Christ, Charlotte!"

"James Madison Nance! Don't take the Lord's whole name in vain like that."

I'm thinking that she's been skimming or something and here I am a Revenooer and might have to go to work for the Zumsari brothers because I'd never let my own flesh and blood take the fall.

"Where'd you get this?"

I can see that she doesn't appreciate my tone but it's too late for that now.

"I saved it. Where'd you think I got it?"

"I don't know. How?"

"God, Jimmy. I ain't a child. I make good money and I don't spend a nickel. You pay for everything."

"What about groceries?"

"Our joint checking account," she says in a says-you voice, which I've got coming.

"What about clothes and stuff?"

"I've bought maybe a thousand dollars in clothes the whole time I've known you. I spend money for gas and supplies. The rest I save. And counting interest that comes to nearly seventy-one thousand dollars. So are we going to build a house or what?"

I'm still dumbfounded. And ashamed. And elated. And if you've ever felt all those things at the same time you know just how weird it is. You want somebody else to do something because you can't. You don't care if they kiss you or kick you, because you're paralyzed.

Charlotte walks over and puts her arms around me.

"We don't have to decide all this tonight," she says.

"Uh-huh."

"I just thought that maybe we could start looking at plans. Maybe think about setting up some kind of time frame."

"Uh-huh."

"Maybe get some people to come in and tell us how much grading has to be done."

"Yeah, we could do that."

See, it's starting to wear off.

"Of course, another fifty cents or so wouldn't hurt," she whispers in my ear.

Then I know I'm getting my legs back. How is none of your business.

"I just saw Mrs. Bocook in a see-through nightie," I answer. "I might be scarred for life."

"Let's see," Charlotte says.

And we do.

And I'm not.

EIGHTEEN

I'm sick the next morning. I'm feverish, my body aches all over and my head feels like I'm in the same orchestra with Tommy Lee. Charlotte wants to stay home with me but I send her on. The sickness isn't in my body. It's in my belly and I know it.

It's time for me to let Ducky go and it's killing me. Maybe all I can do is put away some bad guys for a good stretch and hope that's enough.

Whenever I feel this way, and it isn't often, I have a little ritual. I drive down to the intersection of all the Interstates represented in our fair city, and being the cloverleaf capital of the world you have to know that we've got boodles of Interstates, and the one with the least traffic is the one I take.

All roads lead through Atlanta. You can drive north all the way through Michigan, should your mother-in-law drive you to distraction or you want to see a Pistons' game. You can drive south all the way to Ft. Myers, Florida, and maybe run into Tukey Watson if you get hard-up for a smoke. You can drive west through Birmingham, fast if I were you, and on down to New Orleans, where I would pig-out if I were you. You could drive east to Florence, South Carolina, why, I don't know, and northeast to Charlotte, which contrary to popular belief is named after some old-time Queen and not my love muffin.

And not once would you ever have to leave the Interstate, except on the way to Charlotte I'd stop off in Gaffney, South Carolina, which has a water tower the locals think is shaped like a big peach, but which in reality looks like a fat old derriere with a giant hemorrhoid hanging out.

Me, I take I-75 north and cut off onto I-575 heading northeast.

Monroe's fish camp is out near Lebanon, the town not the country, although if you catch them on a bad day you might not know the difference.

He's got thirty some-odd acres out there with picnic grounds and a couple of hiking trails, a camping area and a little lodge. He's got a six-acre lake that's stocked with bass, catfish and crappie, the last of which is a very nice eating fish even if it is a little boney, and just had the misfortune of having such a ridiculous name.

He's got two one-acre ponds out there stocked with so many bluegill that during the summer you've got about one bluegill per square foot of pond.

We had a radio evangelist once say he had successfully duplicated our Lord's feat (sorry) of walking on water, and it turned out that he had accomplished this on one of Monroe's ponds right after it had been stocked.

He does this on purpose, of course, so that dads can bring their sons out there and catch their limit before the kid's attention span gives out. It also gives wayward yuppies the chance to make a big splash (sorry again) with Junior, so that they can talk about the thrill of the Great Outdoors on the drive home. Naturally Mom won't have any part of it and the poor creatures end up in the garbage can, but at least they got back-to-nature.

And it pays well. You pay by the hour and not by the fish and even though you could catch them with a whistle and a sock everybody seems to feel a sense of accomplishment except maybe the fish.

It reminds me of the time Monroe and a couple of his football buddies saw an ad in the back of one of those hunting magazines for a weekend retreat with a guaranteed kill.

What that means is that you are guaranteed to kill whatever creature is advertised. What that really means is that they've got some poor unsuspecting animals hemmed up somehow just like they were in a cow pasture so that good-old-boys can come in and take potshots at them.

This particular retreat was in the boonies of Florida, which they still have but which are dwindling fast on account of there's more money to be made on Yankees and other foreigners, no offense, and the guaranteed kill was wild hogs.

What they really meant by wild hogs was feral pigs, on account of there aren't any indigenous wild hogs in those parts.

How this occurs is simple. Once upon a time some pigs escaped from their owners. This was back in the days before they had tractors to run them down. Still being pigs, however, they eat and breed and do whatever pigs normally do. Except that in a few generations they were wild, with tusks that will cut you and a disposition toward that very thing. They even turn dark and shaggy just to prove it. So what you've really got is Arnold Ziffel with an attitude.

And the truth is that some guy has got some property with a bunch of these pigs on it, and he knows that they're not going anywhere since they'd have to cross a highway in every direction to do it. So he sees a way to make a buck.

I'm not trying to judge anybody. I just think it would be a lot more sporting if they took away the guns and made the guys go after them with big sticks.

Monroe and his two buddies get an early start the next morning and head out across the cow pasture with their guide, a full-blooded Seminole named McIntyre, go figure, in the lead and their rifles at the ready. The walk until they come to the edge of a cypress swamp.

Cypress are beautiful trees with long trunks and limbs high off the ground, usually laden with Spanish moss. They are often found in shallow water and some of their roots stick up so that the tree can breathe, I guess, and resemble knees. So they call them Cypress knees. And in the old days B.D. (before Disney), every little tourist stop along the road had lamps made out of Cypress knees, though I guess nobody ever stopped to think how the tree felt about this.

The boys look at each other like this is the real thing and

McIntyre moves them into the swamp. They march all morning and don't see a thing except for a few scraggly squirrels which Monroe won't even acknowledge since he's learned his lesson.

Then just before noon McIntyre stops and puts his ear to the wind. He moves them into a little clearing on the tiptoe and they all stop again. Then they hear it. A low grunting that might've been Monroe's stomach rumbling except that they hear a distant thrashing, too, and know Monroe's not a ventriloquist.

They stand at alert, in a circle and back-to-back. If the beast presents himself, he's a goner.

Suddenly this big boar comes charging into the clearing. He's about four hundred pounds with tusks like Samurai sabres. And he's not in a good mood.

McIntyre takes off a dead run and the boar lets him go. Nobody else gets a shot off. Instead each finds the nearest Cypress tree and shinnies up. And inside a minute you've got three NFL football players sitting up on limbs trying to look like that's how they planned it all along...

...while this monster boar circles from one to the other, snorting and grunting and sharpening his tusks on the tree trunks.

"Shoot him!" somebody hollers.

"He's closer to you!" somebody replies.

Monroe adds the voice of reason, which shows you just how desperate the situation was.

"Alright," he says. "Whoever's tree he lights under takes the shot."

They all agree and the boar circles. Finally he picks Monroe, maybe because he smells a little like kinfolk and maybe because the limb he's perched on is only about six feet off the ground.

The boar looks up at him and if you didn't know better you'd swear he smiled.

"Shoot him, Monroe!" his buddies holler.

Monroe tries to steady himself and take aim. The end of his barrel is only about three feet from the boar's head but his hands are shaking so bad he can't shoot.

"Whatchu waiting for?" one asks.

Monroe pauses. "Where should I hit him so's I don't hurt the trophy?"

His two buddies nod. "Good point," they say.

Suddenly the beast loses patience and lunges up at Monroe and gets close enough for Monroe to see that he hasn't been to a dentist lately. Monroe jerks back. Except that there isn't any place for him to jerk back to and instead loses his balance...

"Shoulda let Roadmap baptize me," he mutters.

"Amen," his buddies say.

...and falls out of the tree straight toward that old boar.

They hear the boar grunt and it sounds like *Huh?* and then a loud CRACK! which they think is Monroe's leg.

Nobody opens his eyes for a second and when they do Monroe is kneeling with his hands folded in prayer. The boar is lying beside him and not moving.

Monroe has broken the poor creature's spine and killed him. Once the other two are sure he's dead, which only takes about ten minutes while Monroe pokes him with the butt of his gun, jumps back about ten feet, pokes him again, and then jumps back again, they climb down and start whoopin' and carryin' on.

They got their trophy without firing a shot, and that's how it's remembered.

Except that I've seen the head of that unfortunate critter in Monroe's den. And even the taxidermist with the finest equipment and greatest skill could not get that old boar's eyes uncrossed from where Monroe landed on him.

I pull up to the gate at the fish camp. I usually don't have to pay because I never fish, being family notwithstanding. I just want to take a canoe out on the little lake and paddle around for awhile.

There's somebody I don't know working there. She's a little younger than me and a strawberry blonde, though the strawberry comes from Clairol. She's got a pretty face until she smiles and I see that her two front teeth are headed in opposite directions.

"Hi," I say. "I'm Jim Nance, Monroe's brother."

"Well, hi," she says, and I hate to say it but it's a little hard to watch. "I'm Shirlette, Monroe's new friend. He give me this job. Ain't that sweet of him?"

Uh-oh, I think to myself.

"Beg pardon?" she says.

Uh-oh, I think again. I must've said it out loud.

"I'm pleased to meet you," I say. "I just want to rent a canoe and paddle around the lake a little."

She shakes her head. "He told me you come out here some of the time. It's on the house, same as always."

"Thanks," I say, and then drive off because I'm thinking about asking her if she chewed her pencil a lot in school and nobody stopped her.

I really do like the little lake. It's surrounded by pines and if you've never lived near pine trees you don't know what a comforting hoosh they make when the wind gets up. It's as if the Good Lord wanted to create at least one thing incapable of making a harsh sound.

It's already warm and the only person on the lake is an older guy fishing from the bank at the far end. He doesn't seem to be doing much fishing, really. He's just got his line in so that he'll have something to do while he daydreams. I understand perfectly. That's how I fish. I wave and he waves back and I keep to my end.

I find a place in the sun and lean back and let the canoe drift. The water is very still and I don't drift far.

I know that when I leave here I'm going to have to go back to my office, write my report and submit it. I'm also going to call my buddy at the F.B.I. and let him do the raid. I owe him that.

So I look into the bright blue sky and clear my head of as much noise as I can.

"Sorry, Ducky. I don't know what else to do. But just take

care of yourself now. Make some new friends. Find some peace."

Then a breeze blows through the trees and I hear them whisper to me, although I haven't got the slightest idea what they're saying.

Being out here does remind me of Ben Wright, my old high school principal, though, and the recollection makes me smile as big as the sky. So I decide to stay with Ben a little while.

It seemed at the time that Ben was following me wherever I went. He was my principal in elementary school. When I got to junior high he became the principal there, too. And in high school, sure enough, I looked around at the beginning of my junior year and there was Ben.

It wasn't paranoia. It was probably normal coming from a small school district. In fact, having Ben around so much probably wouldn't have bothered me at all except that he only had one arm.

Nobody ever knew how it happened, though naturally there were rumors. One was that he used to wrestle alligators for a living. Another was that he came to us from a really rough school and a whole gang bushwhacked him once. He beat eight of them to death with his severed arm before he passed out.

In elementary school it was merely threatening. That here was this giant at least five times our size who had a sleeve pinned up where his arm should have been. Junior high is where the stories began. And the names.

The one that met with the most widespread acceptance was Slot Machine. It even became a part of our culture.

I'd see Petey in the hallway looking like he'd had a JuJube flashback, and I'd ask him what was wrong.

"Got caught peekin' up Mary Jo Campbell's dress again," he'd say. "Got to go pay the Slot Machine."

By high school it was really awful.

"Hey," somebody would say. "Ben Wright's the only man I know who swims in circles."

Or we'd be walking down the hall and somebody would see him coming and start humming the theme from *The Fugitive*, and somebody else would call out,

"There he is, Dr. Kimble. Better watch your back."

That one met a long-overdue and merciful end when one day a voice cried out,

"Better watch your back, Hank Kimball!"

I knew that voice, too. It was Monroe.

One day early in my senior year I got called to the office. Slot Machine himself had summoned me.

"You got anything big on today?" he asked.

"No, sir," I said. What'd you expect?

"Good. I want you to go somewhere with me."

My brain took off like a jackrabbit, wondering what crime I'd committed. I'd missed a clutch free-throw against St. Xavier's the year before, but had redeemed myself, with Monroe's help, by draining all the gas out of their bus.

Louise Shepherd broke up with me right after the prom because I couldn't dance like John Travolta and I wrote her phone number on the bathroom wall with the inscription

Call Louise. She's anxious to please.

He signed me out and we took off in his car. We ended up on the Chattahoochee River, which flows west of Atlanta but a long way in both directions. Maybe he was going to drown me just to keep the rest of the school in line.

"You hear about Nance? Slot Machine threw him in the river for calling him Slot Machine."

Turns out, he only wanted to take me fishing. We found a shady spot on the bank with the sweet air of Indian Summer all around us.

Slot Machine wanted to fish for catfish and had brought garden slugs as bait. This in itself is a fairly gruesome proposition, but once your hook was baited and out in the water it was peaceful just to feel the gentle tug of the line as the river ran past.

Watching him was a wonder. He could bait his hook with

just his thumb and forefinger. He could cast like a pro. Then he would stick the handle of the rod behind his calf, keep the rod up with his shin, and work the reel with his hand.

We were both baited and relaxed and he turns to me.

"Seems that I've known you all your life, Jimmy."

"Yes, sir," I said. "I guess it has."

"I need to ask you something."

"Sir?"

"Do we have any problems at school I should know about?"

I wanted to say 'Well, it seems like we've got more than our fair quota of ugly teachers', but I didn't.

"What kind of problems?"

"You know. Drugs. Alcohol. People bringing weapons to school. Things like that."

And then it hit me. He wanted me to be a spy, a fink, a tattletale, a snitch. No wonder I ended up working for the I.R.S.

"Uh, Mr. Wright. You don't want me to be a spy, do you?"

He looked at me like he'd have slapped me a good one if his only hand hadn't been otherwise occupied.

"No, Jimmy, I do not. I'm looking for honesty and I think you'd be honest with me."

I puffed up a little. I couldn't help it.

"Oh. No, sir. Not that I know of."

Which was true. It was a small rural school to begin with and we didn't have those kinds of problems, except a couple of contributions to early motherhood.

"Well, being a principal is sometimes isolating. You don't really get a feel for the things going on around you. Even important things."

I bet it was hard to get the feel for anything with only half your feelers intact, I thought to myself.

"Yes, sir," I said. "But I don't think you've got anything to worry about."

"Especially since Monroe has moved on," he said, and then he grins at me.

I grin back. "Yes, sir."

Then we settle in and here I am ditching school with the principal and thoroughly enjoying myself. He reaches into an ice chest and pulls out a couple of Nehi Oranges and we both start sipping.

I'm also thinking that when we get back to school I'm either going to get beat up a lot or else be the most feared kid around.

"Can I tell you a story?" he asks.

"Sure," I say. Heck, we're buddies now. In an hour I'll be calling him Ben.

"I was with the invasion of France on D-Day. Hitler never knew what hit him 'cause he was expecting us at Calais, but it was still an awful thing once they caught on. The fighting never let up. A bunch of us were hunkered down in a foxhole when a mortar round comes flying in and lands right on top of us. We all know we're dead only it doesn't go off. I'm the closest so I reach down and grab it and fling it as far toward the line as I can. That's when it goes off. And that's the end of the war for me."

"That how you lost your arm?"

Okay, so it was a stupid question, but you've got to remember that I was only seventeen at the time.

"Yes. It was. They gave me a bunch of medals including the Silver Star and shipped me to an Army hospital. Thing is, to keep me from dying they had to take part of my shoulder with the arm. It didn't make all that much difference, really, but it meant I couldn't wear a prosthesis. You know what that is, don't you?"

I nodded. I didn't really, but I figured it had something to do with an artificial arm. And I knew that it was the sorrow of his life, no matter how well he told it.

Then he got a bite and it was a big one. I almost reached to help him but got my hand down before he saw me. He tucked the rod between his thighs and reeled it in. It was about a ten-pound catfish and he was grinning like a kid.

He puts the fish in the bucket and looks over at me.

"There you go, Jimmy. You get back to school you can tell all the kids you went fishing with Slot Machine and he caught a fish *this* big..."

...And then he holds out that single hand of his like half a measurement.

"Jim-my! Jim-my!"

"Sir?"

Then I realize it's not Ben Wright and that I've been dozing. Instead it's Monroe and he's standing at the bank yelling at me. Oh well, it's time to get to work anyway.

I paddle over and he helps me pull the canoe out of the water and into its slot. He seems downright affable today and I don't know what to make of it. The last time he was genuinely nice to me was when he'd just met Shirlene... uh-oh.

"You meet Shirlette?" he asks.

"Yeah. I met her."

"So, whatcha think?"

A part of me wants to ask him how far she can spit, but the look of expectation on his face tells me otherwise. Monroe is a Seeker like everyone else and is only looking for the same connection we all are. And the fact that my opinion is important to him should mean something to me, and sometimes I forget that.

Besides, he looks just like he did the night the Saints drafted him and he got into some clear liquor and had to have his stomach pumped. I can't help but smile.

Maybe brotherhood possesses some inherent qualities after all.

"She seems real nice, Monroe," I say. And I pat him on the back.

NINETEEN

It's late afternoon by the time I get to the office and all I want to do is what I have to do and go home.

I have to fudge a lot in my report since I don't want anybody to know all the specifics of how I came by all the information I have and get the wrong idea. You know and I know, so that's enough.

I begin by saying that I had the misfortune of discovering the body of Clarence 'Ducky' Nash, an informal associate, sorry Ducky, and conducted a cursory investigation of my own.

Subsequent to a visit with Mr. Nash's parole office, Mr. Lee Sharpley, I had a chance encounter with two known associates of Mr. Nash (Dumb Eddie and Slick), and discovered that they, along with several other parolees assigned to Mr. Sharpley, were employed by City Delivery as drivers and/or warehousemen.

I fudge to about a six on the Betty Crocker scale by saying that I observed these two individuals entering their residence with several high-priced consumer items I suspected to be stolen. After additional investigation I determined that City Delivery was central to a major truck hijacking/stolen goods operation, and that all the above named individuals were involved.

I discovered that a truck I observed had been hijacked, taken to the main warehouse of City Delivery during off hours, emptied, the goods stored for an indeterminate period of time and later transferred to another vehicle where they were delivered to a Mr. Henry Bennett of Jacksonville, Florida. I observed what I believe to be monies being exchanged.

I also concluded, with much regret, that Mr Sharpley is one of the leaders of this illicit operation, that an entire series of truck hijackings can be traced to this group, and that as of this writing a quantity of stolen goods can be found in storage at City Delivery's main warehouse in Tucker, Georgia.

I fudged the relationship between Lee and Mrs. Tannenbaum by saying that it is common knowledge, and who could dispute it if doing so would only show their ignorance, that Mr. Sharpley enjoys a personal relationship with the Tannenbaum family, owners of City Delivery as well as many other enterprises.

Then my boss pages me into his office. I don't dread it so much now. I know I'm done and the humidity is low today.

I knock and he waves me in. He has an envelope in his hand and I suspect it's the DMV information I requested on Ducky. I also notice that the corner he's holding has a dark patch that's spread three inches already and hasn't stopped yet.

"Sir?"

"Here's the information you requested. I trust this is the end of it."

"Yes, sir. I just completed my report. I'll give you a copy when I submit it to the proper authorities."

"Good," he says. "I know you're as anxious to get back to work as I am."

I think to myself that I'll never be as anxious as he is and I hadn't stopped working in the first place. Instead I say,

"Yes, sir."

"I trust your interview with Mr. Lee was satisfactory. I haven't gotten his report yet."

"It was fine, sir."

"You seemed to have established a rapport."

"We were both ballplayers in school."

"I see. Well, Mr. Lee is a very important person in the Service. I trust you didn't do anything to embarrass this office."

He just doesn't know any better, does he?

"No, sir," I say. "All went well."

"Good," he says.

Then I move out before the fog starts rolling in. I go back to my desk and open the envelope. I almost laugh out loud. Ducky didn't have a driver's license or a registration for the car. Some things never change and now I'm not so sure they should. I was starting to open Mr. Tannenbaum's envelope when the phone rang.

"Jim Nance."

"This is Colonial Self-Storage," a voice says, and I swear the guy sounds just like Ernest T. Bass.

"What can I do for you, Mr. Bass?"

"Uh, the name's Frankenburger."

"Right. Sorry."

"Anyway, I know you paid your rent six months in advance. But there's been a rate increase, which ain't my fault since I only work here. But if you don't come in and pay the difference by the end of the month we'll have to move your stuff out."

I sit straight up in my chair.

"Wait a minute. You're calling about *my* rent?"

"It's not just you, Mr. Nance. Everybody's rent went up."

"But I rent a space from you."

"Yes, sir. Number 352." He pauses. "This is the Jimmy Nance who's some kind of government agent or something, or am I not supposed to say that on the phone."

"No, it's okay. That's me."

I can feel the key in my pocket begin to glow. I hang up the phone and let out a whoop, which would cause consternation in most cases but nobody here pays any attention since it's me. No wonder I couldn't find it. Ducky used an alias. Me.

I'm still grinning when I open Mr. Tannenbaum's driver's license. It doesn't take me long to stop. Maybe a tenth of a nanosecond.

Instead my mouth falls open like the summer I turned fourteen and was at the community pool, and Judy Watkins, who just turned sixteen, dived off the high dive and lost her top but didn't realize it and then climbs out right in front to me.

The picture on Mr. Tannenbaum's license is somebody we know. Mr Tannenbaum is Lee Sharpley.

Colonial Storage is off the By-Pass on the southeast side of town. Traffic is bad but always seems worse when you're in a hurry, so I put some of my Georgia Driver's Ed to good use and make a lane for myself up the middle. One of the locals gives me the Georgia Peace Sign, but a car from Michigan gives me the thumbs up.

I'm doing seventy-five but my brain is doing ninety. Some of it makes perfect sense. Lee had a double identity, two residences, two cars. Being a parole officer was the perfect cover.

What I didn't understand was the crime. The other businesses were doing well. Why risk it?

I pull up to the gate and see Ernest through the window and wave. He doesn't look anything like Ernest T. Bass. In fact, he looks like Floyd the barber. Funny how things like that work, isn't it?

The place doesn't look very sinister. Just three acres of asphalt with several hundred mini-warehouses of all shapes and sizes perched out there like Outhouses of the Rich and Famous. Number 352 wasn't hard to find. It's in the sixth row right between 351 and 353, just like you'd expect.

I back up to the door so that nobody can see what I'm doing. I see that it's got a padlock that doesn't provide security as much as keep the door from flying off to Kansas the first stiff wind.

My hands are sweating. That's one for you, boss. I try the key in the lock. It fits.

I pull up the door and there it is. A 1981 chopped Eldorado with wire wheels, ground effects and one of those antennae on the trunk lid that looks like a big boomerang. The glass has been tinted so dark you can't see inside.

There's nothing else in the warehouse. No boxes, no trunks, no clues. Whatever Ducky wanted me to see had to be in the car. I catch on fast.

There's no light in the warehouse so I have to use a flashlight. I open the driver's side. The car has shag carpet about a foot thick and even the steering wheel is ringed in the stuff. I pop the glove box. It's empty. There are pockets in the side panels, but they're empty, too.

There's nothing tucked over the visor or under the seats. Except for one of my rainbow Ribbed hidden in the console, the car is empty. Still, it's gratifying to know that Ducky was faithful 'til the end.

Then I see that the keys are in the ignition. I take them and open the trunk. There's a suitcase in there and nothing else. The suitcase isn't locked so I open it.

Holey Moley Judy Watkins!

There are bundles of loot from wall-to-wall, and I think I've been transported to one of those drug movies where the bad guys talk in funny accents and the leader is named Chico. On top of the money is an envelope with my name on it.

The excitement settles and makes a ball in my stomach the size of a cantaloupe, and feels a little like the time Charlotte experimented with one of those *Southern Living* cookbooks and made chicken fried steak.

I hold it for what seemed a long time before opening it.

Finally, I do, and my first impression is that Ducky had really nice handwriting for somebody who walked funny and never had much ambition.

Dear Jimmy,

> *I see you found it. I'm really glad you did but in a way I'm not so glad because I know if you did then that means something bad probably happened to me.*

I stop for a second and sniff. Probably all the dust in the place. I go on.

> *This here is nearly a hundred thousand dollars by my account, but since you're the expert I'll trust your figures.*
> *About half of it is my share from some heists going on, which I'll get to in a minute. The*

other half is money I stole, only I didn't really steal it since it was bad money to start with, or so I figured, and my only intention was to bring it to you when this was all over.

I been working undercover for you the last year and a half and the heists have been going on longer than that. Maybe I shoulda told you about it before now. If I'm dead then I know I shoulda, but I was already on the inside and didn't want to blow my cover.

Oh, Ducky. Why didn't you leave it alone?

Here's one for you. Guess who's running the show? My parole officer, Lee Sharpley. We been taking out trucks and bringing them to the warehouse at City Delivery, where Lee got a bunch of us jobs, and then moving it out again.

Underneath this money is another envelope. It's got the name and number of every truck we took out, and the dates and who did what, just so you know that I wasn't going to take the money and run out on you. If it came to that I was going to let you decide how much I could keep. And I didn't spend any of it either. Except for buying this car, which to be honest is stole to begin with and I couldn't resist.

It's this extra money that caused all the trouble. You remember a guy named Slick, don't you? I know he thinks it's me and he's already causing me grief. That's why I rented this place in your name. I knew you wouldn't let it go.

I always liked you, Jimmy, even if you did have me sent up. I always thought that if the chips was down I could count on you, and that's something I never had my whole entire life.

I just wish I hadn't taken that extra money.

I got no idea why I did.

Your friend,

Ducky.

I'm sniffing pretty loud. Maybe my reaction to Charlotte's muscadine jelly has kicked in. I wipe my eyes with my sleeve and try to clear my throat.

"Shit, Ducky," I say. "You should've come to me."

"Now ain't that touching," a voice says behind me. And I won't lie to you. It spooks me good.

I turn and see Dumb Eddie and Slick standing in the doorway and their expressions are genuinely unfriendly. So are the expressions of the guns they've got pointed at me. Slick has a little snub-nose .38 but Eddie's got a .44 the size of a rooster.

I couldn't believe me own stupidity.

"You followed me?"

"Boy, you are just one dumb hick," Slick says. "We knew you were followin' us around. That truck of yours sticks out like a sore foot."

"Thumb," I say.

Which was not a very smart thing to do since it only makes him mad.

"Yeah, well be a wise-ass all you want. I figure you got about an hour to get it out of your system."

I look at Eddie. He's trying to look mean but I can see he's confused. Maybe that's the way he looks all the time this close up, I don't know. But I had the feeling that when he was filling out his application for vocational school murder wasn't his first choice.

"That how you feel about it, Eddie?"

He seems impressed that I'd even ask. But all he did was point the rooster at me and wave it outside.

"Let's move," he said.

They put Eddie in the van with me and Slick followed in the Gremlin. Frankly I was relieved I didn't have to ride in it. Slick took Ducky's suitcase, though, and locked the warehouse again.

I was scared but knew it wouldn't help to show it. I was angry but helpless, so all that was left was charm.

"Where to?" I ask.

And if you'd heard me you'd think I was taking Dumb Eddie for a little buzz through the country.

"Warehouse," he said. "And no funny stuff."

"You got it."

I felt a little better because I didn't think they'd shoot me in the warehouse. Maybe they were just going to hold me hostage. Charlotte's got almost two hundred dollars in quarters. Maybe they wanted help with their taxes. Maybe they were going to have Spud take me out in the woods and whack me.

But I was betting on meeting somebody there. Mr. Big. At least that would give me a little more time to figure something out.

We hit the Interstate toward Tucker and I see Slick in the rear-view following close.

"Looks like a cloud moving in," I say, looking up at the sky.

Out of the corner of my eye I see Eddie look, and figure that's a good sign. So I sigh with all the resignation I can muster and put on my most sincere voice. The one I'd use if I worked for Public Radio.

"You know, Ducky was my friend. All I want to know before this is over is why'd you kill him, Eddie?"

Eddie sat stone still and didn't make a sound, except for a faint, muffled screech like rusty gears, which I figure is Eddie's brain trying to figure out what I'm up to.

"I mean, he took money that didn't belong to him and that ticked people off. I understand that. But you knew him. All you'd have to do is give him a big Boo! and he'd be in the next state. You didn't have to go and cut him up like that."

Then I shake my head in woe, which wasn't all acting.

"I didn't kill nobody," Eddie says.

"Maybe not. But you were there, weren't you? And you're going to take the fall for it just like always. Even if they don't catch you right away, there isn't a statute of limitations on murder."

"Hey, I could care less about statues of limitations," he said.

And I flash on Miss Liberty up in New York Harbor with a tablet that reads 'Give me your tired, your poor, your limited'.

I lower my voice another notch, which isn't easy.

"How many times you gone away for Slick already, Eddie. Four? And this isn't six months in County for snatching watches. This is big-time stuff. This is death row stuff."

I see him shift a little so I pour it on. "You ever hear about what happens to a guy when they throw that switch?"

"Sheeuh," he scoffs at me. "You think they'd throw the switch on me for not even doing it?"

"Accessory is still murder-one in Georgia, Eddie."

"Hey, Mr. Smarty-smart. Look at that A-rab that whacked Bobby Kennedy that time. If anybody deserved the long one he did. And he's still alive, ain't he? And sooner or later they're gonna have to let him out when he gets too old to do no harm."

It's hard to argue with logic like that.

"Well, this is Georgia. And a different time. And even if you're right, you want to spend your whole life in hard time just because Slick couldn't control his temper?"

He looks at me quick and his face turns red. But instinct takes over and he just waves the rooster at me.

"Shut up," he says. And that's good enough for me.

We get to the warehouse and park around back. Slick has a key and unlocks the back door. He motions me in.

"Where's Spud?" I ask.

"Who?" says Eddie.

"He means the guard, you craphead," Slick says. "We gave him the night off just to give you some privacy. Now move it."

I start moving across the floor toward the stairway leading to the loft. I don't want to think it, but I'm beginning to think that they are going to shoot me right here in the warehouse. I close my eyes for a second and wish Charlotte good-bye. I tell her how she saved me and how I'm sorry if I didn't let her know that in all the right ways.

Then something strange happened. I hear Slick and Eddie talking under their breaths behind me, and if I didn't know better I'd swear they were arguing.

Slick's voice was sharp and nasty, and Dumb Eddie sounded hurt but assertive. Then it gets louder and I sneak a peek to see Slick standing in Eddie's face and Eddie not giving an inch, with both of them waving their guns for emphasis.

"I ain't in no more," Eddie said. "I ain't goin' on Death Row for nobody."

"He's a Fed, for God's sake," Slick sneered. "He can already put you away forever."

We're near the stairway when Slick finally pushes Dumb Eddie aside, and then turns toward me all tense and generally upset.

"You dumb bastard!" he says, which if I were in a position to I'd tell him he was only half-right. "Filling his head with all kinds of shit. I ought to pop you right now!"

I put my hands up quick. I've got nothing to lose now and I know it.

"All I said was that he shouldn't have to take any more falls for things he didn't do."

"What?" Slick said, and it was halfway between a shriek and a whine. "What the Hell are you talking about?"

"About all the times Eddie's gone up while you stayed out and lived it up. The cops know it. They also know you killed Ducky and are just waiting for you to step the wrong way. And I don't think it's right for you to take Eddie with you."

"And maybe if we pop you we'll all stay out," he says.

Good point.

"See, that's exactly what I'm talking about. You're already history, Slick. Eddie's looking at five years tops. But you can't stand that. You're going to take him down, too, because the real truth is, you don't give a flying flip about him."

"That's it!" he ranted. "I've had it with your stupid, nosey butt!" And I'm not about to correct his metaphor. "You're done, snoop!"

And with that he looks at Eddie.

"Do him now."

Eddie seemed stunned, which wasn't much of a stretch.

"Uh, what?"

"Do him now. Close his mouth for good."

"Ain't we supposed to wait?" Eddie protested.

"I said do him now!"

"Whyn't you do him?"

"You turning chicken shit? Is that it?"

"Then it's over for you, Eddie," I pipe up. Hey, you think I'm just going to stand there? "You really will be guilty then."

Slick boils over like a spoiled kid and pushes Eddie toward me, which is more than a respectable feat.

"Do, him Eddie!"

"I don't want to."

Ah, Eddie. That monolith of moral courage.

"I said do him now, you big gob!"

"No."

"Do what I tell you!"

For maybe the first time in his life, Eddie is determined.

"No, Slick. I ain't."

"Do it!"

"Nope."

"I said do it!"

"Nope."

Slick completely lost it then. Whatever flimsy ganglia held his neuro-transmitters together snapped with a Crack! and a Hi-Ho Silver!

He slapped Eddie hard in the face. I could see the tears well in Eddie's eyes.

"Do it!"

"No."

Another slap.

"Do it!"

"No."

He stood so close they breathed the same air.

"I said shoot, you fat worthless piece of puke! SHOOT!!!!!"

So he did.

TWENTY

I smelled the cordite hanging in the air and I heard the echo of the gunshot fade.

But I didn't see Ducky, Allan Pinkerton or even Elvis. So I opened my eyes.

And what I do see is Slick lying on the concrete floor with a big, meaty red hole where his left eye used to be. Eddie is standing over him blubbering, which is scary to see, and then he turns toward me.

"You made me do it," he says, choking back sobs. "You son-of-a-bitch, you made me do it."

I nodded, mainly because he was waving the rooster again.

"I didn't do it on purpose, Eddie," I said, which was true. "I'm sorry." Which wasn't.

"Yeah, well you're gonna be," he says, pulling himself together and moving in my direction.

I see the barrel of Slick's gun sticking out from under the palm of his hand. It's my only chance and so I hold my hands up in complete surrender and move slowly toward the body, nodding all the while as if he's got me dead-to-rights, which may be an unfortunate choice of words, I know, but applicable.

"Just let me see if maybe he isn't still alive," I said.

Eddie looks at me and his eyebrows shoot up, like somebody had just told him there wasn't no Easter Bunny and I'm a good pal who says it ain't so. Still, he waggles the rooster at me and I'm worried it might cock-a-doodle-doo on its own.

"All I'm going to do is feel for a pulse," I say.

Eddie nods and gives me permission. I see his eyes squench in concentration. He's watching my hand all the way and I slowly reach to feel Slick's neck. I already know that he's deader than the Honeymoon Suite at the St. Petersburg Hilton, but that's not the point. The point is that Eddie hasn't taken his eyes off my left hand, which gives me the opportunity to put my right hand down on top of Slick's gun and palm it.

Now I know for a fact how Dumb Eddie got his nickname.

I feel for a pulse and make it look good. Then I slowly stand up, holding my left hand out to my side as far as it will reach. Eddie's eyes follow it like he's been tranced, which allows me to gently shove Slick's .38 into my back pocket.

I'd be proud of myself if I hadn't had to put the gun in nose-down, which means that if it goes off unexpectedly I'll have a couple of new dimples where I don't especially want them.

Eddie's looking at me expectantly but there's nothing I can do now but play it out.

"He's gone, Eddie."

He looks at me and nods as if I've done my best.

We hear the outside door open and close and we both know we've got company. I can't make a move yet and so the only thing for me to do is leave it to Eddie, which is not a very comforting thought.

"You can still walk away from this, Eddie. You get me out now and I'll do everything I can to help you."

He stares at me for a second and I think he's seriously considering it. Finally he just shakes his head.

"Naw," he says.

Then I see Lee Sharpley walking across the floor toward us. He's smirking at his superior intelligence and my misfortune until he gets close enough to see that Slick is not merely resting.

"What the Hell?"

"It was an accident, Mr. Sharpley," Eddie explains, back to being the lap dog. He looks to me to back him up and I oblige him. Why the Hell not?

"Yeah," I said. "It was an accident."

Lee hasn't even made eye contact yet.

"Go back to the supply room and find the postal bags. The big ones."

"Yes, sir," Eddie says.

Then Lee looks at me and I see the face of whatever turned him.

"Bring two," he says.

Eddie nods and starts to hotfoot it away.

"Eddie?" Lee calls after him.

"Sir?"

"The gun."

"Oh, right," Eddie says sheepishly, then hands the rooster to Lee before hotfooting it away again.

Lee looks at me and I see a slight discomfort in how he holds the gun. It's like the foreman of a road crew. He's good at walking back and forth and barking out orders while the other guys sling their picks and shovels, but put a shovel in his hands and he cuts off his own toes.

I keep my hands up, though. Even if Lee is as bad a shot as I am he's close enough to kill me.

"So," he says. "Jim Nance."

I play to his ego. It gives me time to think.

"How long have you known?" I ask.

He grins. "Since the beginning," which I knew to be a lie but you think I'd call him on it? "After that day you showed up in my office I did some checking. Found out Ducky was your snitch. Then Slick saw you following him. You watch too much T.V., Jimmy."

I shrug. What else could I do.

"Killing Ducky wasn't too smart," I said.

He nods and gives Slick a quick glance. I couldn't tell if Slick looked back or not but the odds are against it.

"Yeah, Slick was a maniac. I just wanted him scared off and the money back. Slick had other plans, I guess."

"As you do," I say.

"Yeah. I do."

"I hate to sound cliché, but people will look for me."

"I know. But by the time anybody really knows what's going on I'll be long gone."

And then he smiles as if he knows something nobody else knows, except that I think I know what it is and he doesn't know that.

Instead I play it dumb, which isn't Oscar-worthy, I admit, but same to you.

"How'd all this happen, Lee?"

And if you'd heard me you'd think we were best buddies and I'd just caught him sneaking around on his girlfriend.

"It started back in college," he says. And I hate to say I told you so, but I told you so. "It started small and just got bigger. It got so big that one of the guys who worked it with me set up a network in Florida to move the stuff."

"Henry Bennett," I say. Sorry, I couldn't help myself.

He's surprised but doesn't want to let on. "So you know about him. Congratulations."

I shrug again. No point rubbing it in.

"It got so big in fact that we decided to set up some kind of legitimate business to run everything through. So I bought this place."

He's too cocky for me, rooster or not.

"You mean you invented Eric Tannenbaum and Eric Tannenbaum bought this place."

Okay, so if he shoots me now we'll both know why.

He's surprised and can't hide it. His mind is working quick now, wondering if his tracks are still covered, wondering if anybody else knows, and looking at me like I've taken his sister out and didn't bring her home 'til dawn and am smoking a cigarette when I let her out of the car. But eventually he tries to shrug it off.

"So you figured it out."

"It wasn't that hard."

"No?"

"Un-uh. The socks gave you away."

This irks him and his cheeks tighten, and along with them,

his grip. I don't want him out of control, so I help him out a little. And I do it so it won't sound like I'm as smart as he is.

"Being a parole officer was the perfect cover. It gave you a squeaky clean reputation and access to a work force who wouldn't dare cross you."

He gives me about an eighth of a nod and I move on.

"But you had too much money for a parole officer so you invented Eric Tannenbaum. As Eric you hired some good lawyers and set up a corporate structure that nobody could get through and a few foreign bank accounts. Then you bought this place and operated it as a legitimate company while sending the bad bucks overseas, where I presume they are waiting for you in case you decide to take an early retirement."

"Very good, Jimmy."

"The only thing I don't understand is why all the other companies?"

He smiles a little as if he doesn't understand it himself.

"You know what's funny about that? This place made money hand-over-fist. I couldn't believe it. So I bought other companies, and they made money hand-over-fist."

"So why not get out of the rackets?" Sorry, maybe I do watch too much television.

"Too much invested," he says. "Too easy."

"So you've got what, four-five million stashed somewhere?"

"Try eight," he says, and is feeling his oats again. "And I don't even have to sneak. Old Eric's passport is as legal as you, Jimmy boy."

"And while everybody back here is trying to figure out the mess you made, you and Mrs. Tannenbaum will be on a nice beach somewhere."

He sours at this and I don't know why.

"Mrs. Tannenbaum can fend for herself," he says, and it's not sentimental by a long shot.

Then it made sense. All the running between the apartment and the house, the two sets of clothes, not counting the socks, the two cars. It wasn't just a cover. Mrs. Tannenbaum really thinks she is Mrs. Tannenbaum. She doesn't know Lee Sharpley from Snuff Waldrep. Even after all I know, this offends me.

"Jeez, Lee. She's your wife."

"And you're stalling," he says tersely. "I think that about finishes our business."

I see Eddie coming back across the warehouse dragging two large bags, one of which is intended for me. I don't want to spend eternity in a mailbag. It's now or never.

"I'll give you a head start," I say, and I'm all business.

"What?" And naturally he's incredulous.

"You can leave me here with Eddie and I'll try to work things out with him."

"God, you are one stupid Cracker. Why would I do that?"

"Because that passport isn't going to do you one bit of good. You think I'd sit on this stuff? My people know who you are and the F.B.I. knows who you are."

He's had it easy for so long that he's started to feel invulnerable and it's made him a little crazy.

"You're full of shit."

"How do you think I found out?"

He looks at me then and he's worried.

"Your driver's license, Lee. Eric Tannenbaum's driver's license has your picture on it. I faxed it to the F.B.I. right before I left the office. Call your house. See if you haven't had some uninvited visitors. I'm surprised they haven't raided this place yet."

I'm bluffing but he doesn't know it. In fact, I put my report and all the rest of it in my lap drawer before I left. By the time they get it all figured out I'll have been chasing bad guys in heaven for six months and Lee'll have a first-rate tan.

But he believes me and the fury in his face is the same I saw in Slick's. Maybe there is a criminal consciousness after all. And once it's gotten to you it does something to your spirit.

Eddie arrives huffing and puffing and Lee is glaring at me.

"Put Slick in the bag," he says.

Eddie gives him a pitiful look but does what he's told. I can't bear to watch, except that when it's over I see a spot of coagulated blood on the floor.

Then he hands the rooster back to Eddie.

"Do it," he says, and it's mean and low and full of breath.

"Sir?" Eddie asks.

"I said do it."

"Here?"

"Now!" Lee says.

Eddie thinks for a second. "Why not outside?"

"Somebody will hear," Lee says through clenched teeth. "Do it now."

Eddie pauses again. Maybe he's tired of doing everybody else's dirty work. Maybe he understands in his own way that life possesses an intrinsic sanctity and value. Maybe he didn't get enough sleep last night.

Either way, I've been through this before and can't depend on lightning to strike twice. Hey, I've got more at stake than anybody. I jump in.

"Eddie know you're getting ready to get on a plane and leave him here holding the bag?" Sorry again.

"What?" Eddie says.

"God damn it," Lee rants. "Just shoot the son-of-a bitch!"

"Eddie know about Eric Tannenbaum, Lee? About how you set up a secret identity that's going to allow you to just waltz out of the country?"

"Is that true, Mr. Sharpley?" Eddie says, turning a little toward him.

"You dumb bastard. Just shoot him!"

With Eddie turned I've got no choice. Dear Lord, why was I born with such an intolerance of guns. Why didn't I spend more time at the range?

Eddie's still looking at Lee with a worrisome expression but my gut says it won't last. He is an automaton and moves in whatever direction he's pushed, and I can see that Lee has a far greater hold on him than Slick ever did. If he looks my way again, I'm dead. I can feel it.

I see his head start to turn. I reach behind me and feel the butt of the gun tight against...well, my own butt. The rooster is up and ready to crow even if Eddie hasn't aimed yet. I slip my finger on the trigger so that I won't have to fumble once it's out of my pocket, hoping that I don't shoot myself in the process and die in utter shame.

I can see the Coroner's report now. *One shot to the head. One to the ass.*

Eddie's eyes move toward me. The rooster moves with him. I can almost see the tendons flex on his trigger finger.

My only chance is to get him on the uptake. I whip the gun up and away from my body. Eddie points. I nose the gun up and fire in the same motion...

...a shot explodes!

I catch Eddie in the hand and see the gun fall as he instinctively jerks his hand up and holds it to his chest.

"Ow," he says.

I think about Ducky up in heaven with Randolph Scott and when they see me they start giving each other low-fives. Except that the sad truth is I was aiming at Dumb Eddie's chest, since it's the widest target, and would have killed him if it came to that. Sorry, Eddie. But what's the harm in letting Ducky have a moment of pride.

Then I see Lee edging toward the gun. I take a step forward and kick it across the floor. I point my gun directly at his head and cock it for emphasis.

"Lee."

He looks at me and knows it's over. I smile. I can't help it.

"Don't count that chicken 'til your fingers need lickin'."

AFTERWORD

The F.B.I., sans Herschel Walker, swooped in and put even the Fireman's Drag Races to shame. My buddy is so happy that he gives me a big hug right in front of everybody. Why not? He'll be in Washington with the big boys because of this.

Everybody gets a hoot out of how I secured the suspects. I made them take off their belts, and seeing that there was such a disparity between them, I used Eddie's belt to tie up Lee, which went around his chest twice and still buckled, and I used Lee's belt to tie Eddie's hands behind him.

I give them every piece of evidence I have and with Ducky's journal the case is made. They keep me out of all the press and hoopla because of my cover, but I don't mind. I want it that way. I do see to it that Ducky's name gets mentioned as a key player in the investigation, for which he lost his life.

The Service does see fit to give me the Medal of Valor, though, which is the highest award it has. They do it privately, but it's still very nice. Tommy Lee flies down to bestow it on me himself. Charlotte's there and cries from pure pride.

They're going to take a picture to run in the Service's paper but my boss insists on being in it and the lens keeps fogging up—even the wide-angle one they have to change to.

I feel a little responsible for Eddie since I almost killed him, even if he doesn't know it, and find him a good lawyer. Eddie rolls on everybody. I vouch that Slick's death was in self-defense and that I believed whole-heartedly that Slick killed Ducky.

He'll do a solid fifteen years but he'll still be alive when he gets out. He even makes a point to thank me and asks me to come see him in prison, which I promise to do.

Lee Sharpley/Eric Tannenbaum hired a big gun but eventually rolled over, too. He gave them details of every heist going back nearly ten years, and an accounting of all the money, just to be free of the murder implications.

He'll do twenty-five years minimum and be way past his prime when he gets out.

The law never even has to break a sweat.

We seized all his corporate and personal assets. Except that they are all so profitable, and with the government's cash flow not what it should be, everyone thought it best to leave the businesses intact.

Mr. Delray is now running City Delivery and calls me about every other day to thank me. I tell him I had very little to do with it.

I got Arnold Carvey into a summer league at the Y and the last I heard he was tearing it up. He's already got some private schools after him with full scholarships.

I turned down the job in Washington. Charlotte and I are looking at plans for the house and doing our best to keep them from Mrs. Bocook. We don't want her to know how much garage space we'll have.

Slick's dead, so I guess that's all the justice Ducky could hope to expect.

There was one item of business I took care of in person, though I wasn't looking forward to it. I drove out to the Tannenbaum's one afternoon wearing my coat and tie, and when I knocked on the door she answered.

She didn't recognize me at first, and when she did she didn't know whether to smile or claw my eyes out. She finally smiled, but there was a lot of pain there. I understood. I was responsible.

"I just wanted to see you and tell you I'm sorry," I said.

She shrugged. "You were just doing your job, I guess."

"Well, I wouldn't stand on that if I'd hurt an innocent person."

She looks me up and down. "No. I don't think you would."

I nod and beg my leave. If I'd been wearing a hat I'd have tipped it.

"Officer," she calls after me.

It should be Agent but I'm not going to correct her.

"Jim," I say.

"You have anything to do with me being allowed to keep my house?"

I shrug. "Can't very well put a lady out into the street," I say.

"Thanks," she said. "I can get a good stake out of this house. I'm moving to Florida. I'm too old to work for a living again."

It wasn't age and we both knew it. But who was I to judge. She'd bought into something that was a lot less real than even she had allowed herself to believe. I wasn't going to tell her differently.

"Take care of yourself," I say.

"You, too," she answers.

The only thing nobody else knows about is that I confiscated $4000 from Ducky's suitcase before the Feds got there. I won't try to justify myself except to say that I got Ducky's ashes out of hock and bought him a very nice spot in a mausoleum at Hillcrest, which is one of the city's finer resting places.

I invited everybody I knew and they all showed up. It let me know just what good friends I have. Rudy and his wife came. Charlotte was there, of course, but so were my folks. Even Mrs. Bocook came.

Monroe came with Shirlette and I saw them holding hands. She didn't open her mouth much so that was okay. Arnold and his whole family came. Tommy Lee stayed over an extra day to be there and spent some time with Charlotte and me at the house.

But when Miss Eva sang *Sweet Hour of Prayer* there wasn't a dry eye to be found. Even Monroe started bawling.

So I guess that's about it. Everything got back to normal pretty fast. To tell you the truth, I'm glad. I'm back on my route full time and one of the first things I did was have Flora Watkins popped again, bless her heart.

Oh, about Ducky's car. I decided to keep it. For old times sake.